Allow yourself to fall
into these stones, as they
were written for you,

forever

THE STORM

AKEEM BALOGUN

OKAPI BOOKS

Okapi Books
Level 6, Aspect Court, Sheffield. South Yorkshire, S1 2BG
okapibooks.com

Cover painting, 'The Storm', and story title page art
by Arantza Pardo

Cover design by Nathan Ryder at Ryder Design

The copyright acknowledgements on page 241
constitute an extension of this copyright page.

Typesetting by Bracketpress

Printed and bound in England by TJ Books Ltd.,
Trecerus Industrial Estate, Padstow, PL28 8RW

A CIP record for this book is available
from the British Library.

ISBN 978-1-8380441-0-7 [paperback]
ISBN 978-1-8380441-1-4 [hardback]

For you, the reader

Akeem Balogun was born in Hammersmith, London, 1991, and spent his early years in Brixton. He presently lives in Sheffield, South Yorkshire. *The Storm* is his first book.

This title is also available as an audiobook narrated by Rider Shafique.

Contents

The Storm	1
Eden	27
Seize	41
Marc Populaire	55
Benjamin's Mansion	69
Soulmate	107
A Stroke of Madness	113
Room Four	144
An Ill Wind	157
Bonfire Hero	163
Cold Expressions	181
Buddhatarium	189
The Weatherman	213

The Storm

The cold metal of Seun's zip pushed against his chin as he tucked his head into the mouth of his coat. His body was tense against the chill, and his large hood veiled his vision. Whenever the storm weakened, he would glance around and see handfuls of people behind scarves or with umbrellas, arching their bodies forward so that they were shaped like spears cutting through the wind. Each time the storm reignited, Seun would turn his back to it so that petals of rain didn't find their way through the shield of his hood. He took cover in the recess of the entrance to his workplace. Seconds later, he heard the door click. The blurred window meant he wasn't able to see who was behind it, but he knew it was Grace from how fast it was being opened. She yelled something he couldn't hear over the weather. She shouted again, 'Why are you out here?'

She reached forward and pulled him through the door before shutting it once he was inside. She was smiling. 'Why do you do that? Why not have your break inside with everyone else?'

Seun looked from Grace's camo raincoat down to her black jeans and knee-high boots. She was watching him. 'We can't stay inside forever,' he said.

Grace's smile faded. 'We might have to.'

Inside the office, people were sitting facing their computers or talking to the person next to them. As they worked, they tried to ignore the noise of the storm, which was inconsistent; often, rain pummelled the windows in bursts, while other times it was serene – a calming stream of noise – but what would follow was always worse and struck with such force it made the building tremble. If anyone spoke during these overpowering moments it felt offensive, and the others would frown at the speaker to indicate that they should be silent – as if to speak during the storm's most vicious moments was to talk over God.

On the office whiteboard, Seun was writing a list of the stationery they needed.

Callum, who was sitting at the back of the room, noticed. 'Mate, don't even bother. Deliveries have been here and there for days now.'

'We need to keep a record for when the storm's over,' Seun replied.

Callum stared at him. He chuckled. 'Alright then.'

Seun finished the list and went back to his desk.

At 1pm, Callum turned the TV on. The entire office waited for the weather forecast. When it started, the department manager, Louise, leaned out of her room to get a better look. Seun focused on the weatherman. It had been the same one for the past few days. He now seemed tired, and Seun thought that in his eyes there was a hopelessness that hadn't been there yesterday. The team watched as he described the patterns of the coming days; on the map of the nation, most areas were covered in grey cloud, and he urged anyone remaining in the west region of Wrentpole to follow the evacuation and head east or south and not to risk travelling to Cahringham or Holmechester. He went on to say that the storm would worsen as the week progressed but should finally give way soon after.

'It's going to get worse before it gets better?' Callum said. 'Is he serious? It's been hell for nearly two weeks in a row now.'

There were mumbles of agreement, followed by talk about trees being uprooted and cars being turned over.

'I can't sleep,' Louise added. 'Thank God the kids can, through anything, but at night it sounds like there's a—'

'Monster,' said Callum. 'How many dead now? Two thousand?'

No one spoke.

'They've stopped counting,' Seun said. Everyone focused on him. 'The authorities probably don't know the figure themselves. I doubt they've been back to the worst-hit areas since the storm started, and I don't blame them. It's not like it's subsided.'

Louise stepped forward. 'Does anyone still have family in the west?'

Seun's colleagues shook their heads. A few said that any friends and family they had there left following the evacuations. Louise's eyes scanned the room. Knowing he wouldn't be able to answer as casually as the others, Seun said nothing and focused on his screen as he felt Louise's gaze cross him. The sound of the storm rose, and the lightning that followed changed the subject.

After everyone had left, Seun remained to catch up on some work. When he'd finished, he put his coat and gloves on and made his way out. Daytime was fading. He jogged to his car, which was parked near a busy road, and got inside. Once behind the wheel, he edged forward as headlights zoomed past along with the sound of rainwater scattering beneath tyres. When there was a gap in the traffic, he accelerated onto the road, ignoring the speed limit like everyone else, in order to get home before nightfall.

By the time he reached his house it was dark. He forced his door shut against the wind, turning the noise of the storm into a muffled howl, before making his way upstairs. Thunder echoed. When he reached the top, his phone rang. He answered.

'What's up?'

Khensy laughed at the other end of the line. Seun could barely hear her due to the poor signal.

'That's a lazy greeting. How are you?'

Seun was now walking along the upstairs passageway. 'You know how I am: home alone, but otherwise I'm okay.'

'You're making me feel bad.'

Seun leaned against the banister. He rubbed his eyes. 'Sorry. I don't mean to.'

'Just be patient, please?'

'I'm trying. It's been weeks since I last saw you.'

'I know, but once the storm's calmed—'

'And when will that be?'

Khensy didn't answer.

'This is what I said in the beginning; we live too far apart.'

The connection worsened, and when Khensy replied, Seun had to ask her to repeat herself – twice.

'I said stop saying that. It can work. Do you think I like being stuck in my parents' house? It was fine before this fucking weather started, wasn't it?' Her voice thinned. 'And now it's going to ruin everything.'

Seun shook his head. 'It's always been a problem.'

Khensy sighed. 'Anyway, how's your dad?'

'You're changing the subject.'

'Is he okay?'

Seun fell silent. He glanced upwards at the ceiling. 'I haven't heard anything from him.'

'Nothing? It's been two days.'

'I know … I might go over.'

'What? Are you crazy?'

'I'm not, but no one's searching for anyone in this weather. Look how many people have gone missing already. It's been forty-eight hours – who knows what's happened to him.'

'… You're not being serious. Think about what you're saying, please.'

'I am.' Seun felt his voice crack. 'I can't wait—' The signal deteriorated and the phone cut off.

Straight away Seun's mobile lit up, showing him a message: Reception's crap. Don't be stupid. Stay put.

When he got to his room his phone chimed: And I'll come as soon as the storm ends.

He ignored it.

It wasn't until a few hours later, when he was in bed and about to sleep, that he replied: Okay.

DAY 12

In the morning, Seun could tell by the thrum of the wind outside that it was calmer than it had been for the past several days. Outside his window, the trees weren't bending back against the wind and only litter was being pulled through the air – not bins or shop signs. He grinned and reached for his boots.

Out in the cold, Seun had his hood on tight, and what would have been a five-minute drive was taking him an hour-long walk in the storm. He struggled to glimpse ahead as he forced himself through it. Around him, others were doing the same. He managed to get a good look at one of them, and when they saw each other they laughed.

'You're late,' said Louise.

Grace stood up. 'I was going to text you and ask where you were.'

'I walked to work.' Seun closed the door behind him. He saw Louise roll her eyes. 'It was lighter than it's been. We should enjoy these moments.'

'That was stupid of you,' Louise said. 'It's still strong enough to take you off your feet. But that's just like you.' She chuckled sarcastically. 'Accept defeat, Seun. This is the weather we're talking about.'

'Don't be so bleak,' he said.

'How am I? The storm's here for the time being, and we're going to have to live accordingly – not take risks like you have.'

'But—'

'Next time, drive, or at least get public transport – if it's running.'

Seun turned his back to her and headed to his desk. He noticed Callum glance at him, and then at Grace, who was still standing, then back at him, and then at Grace once more.

Callum leaned over his desk and whispered at Grace loud enough for Seun to hear, 'Why did you get up when Seun walked in?'

Grace's face turned red, and she quickly sat down. As Callum giggled, someone shouted and pointed, making everyone focus in the direction they were aiming at; through the window and behind the clouds, the sun was showing.

'Oh my God,' Grace shouted. 'How long's it been since we've seen that?'

Everyone cheered.

By lunchtime, the sun had disappeared.

The change in people's moods was almost instinctive; during lunch, Seun found Grace less talkative than she had been only a half an hour ago and himself the same. After what was a quiet break with little speaking amongst anyone, Seun was back by his desk and staring through the window beside him. He looked away from the darkening clouds and his eyes met Grace's. She gave him a weak smile before lightning flashed.

Seun stayed late. Once everyone had gone, Grace, who was sitting at the other end of the office, got up and headed over to him. She pulled out a chair and took a seat beside him.

'Not in a rush to go?' Seun asked.

Grace shook her head. 'You walking back home?'

Seun glanced at the rain outside. 'Definitely not.'

Grace shifted in her seat. 'Do you have any family in the west?'

'Yeah, my dad.'

'Have you heard anything from him?'

'No, not yet. But the reception must be terrible. He'll get back to me.'

Grace watched him type. She was about to say something else when the door opened, and everyone who had left a few minutes ago trooped back in.

'Jesus,' Callum said. 'We're sleeping here tonight.'

Seun got up from his desk. 'Is it that bad?'

Callum laughed. 'Bad? We wish. It's something else. We couldn't even walk through it. Check outside.'

Seun peered out of the window and realised the rain was attacking the glass harder than it had been a moment ago.

Louise came in last and shut the door behind her. 'There should be some sleeping bags in the storeroom. Bring 'em up if you want. I'm staying in my office.'

The rest of them watched Louise head to her room and close the door.

'Surely it'll get better?' asked Grace.

'Not according to the forecast,' Callum answered. He sat down at his desk and nodded to his computer. 'Can we get streaming services on these?'

They agreed to sleep by 10pm and to head back home early the next day, which was a Saturday. A group of them went into the storeroom while others collected some cushions from the couches in the reception area. After everything had been brought up, Seun helped Grace with a sleeping bag.

Callum, who was watching them, said, 'Grace and Seun are sharing the same bag everyone, so there's a spare for anyone who wants it.'

Grace frowned at Callum, and as Seun studied his colleagues, he knew they wanted to maintain a professional manner but had lost it to the storm, and he couldn't help chuckling when they all laughed.

When they were ready to sleep, the office lights were switched off except for a desk lamp. Someone spoke, and immediately Callum said, 'Knew it was going to be difficult to get a good night's sleep here.'

'Keep quiet,' Grace whispered.

'And Louise is too good to sleep with the rest of us,' he added.

'I can hear you,' Louise said from inside her office.

'Can she?' Seun asked as he tried to stifle his laughter.

'And I heard that as well,' she said.

'Wow,' said Callum, 'her ears must be—'

'Shut up,' Louise shouted.

Seun laughed, and the others joined him. They only quietened when multiple blue flashes of lightning appeared, followed by thunder.

'How are we meant to sleep through this?' Grace said.

'Well,' replied someone in the darkness, 'if you keep your mouth shut, we might stand a chance.'

A few people chuckled, including Seun. He couldn't see

Grace, but he could tell from the sound of her moving that she had rolled over to face him and was probably glaring in his direction.

Callum spoke, 'I'm starting to forget what a good day looks like.'

'Don't say that,' said Grace. 'It will end.'

'Will it?' Callum asked. 'They were saying that two weeks ago. Imagine how much damage it's caused now. Imagine how many people have actually died – they still don't know the figure.'

'Christ, Callum,' Louise shouted.

'Sorry … How badly do you think this is affecting wildlife?' Callum whispered. 'Or farming – the whole food industry even?'

'It can't be good,' Seun answered. 'I'm starting to see empty shelves in the supermarket. The fear is real.'

'Maybe the storm's a weapon,' Grace said quietly.

Everyone fell silent.

'I mean, maybe the government's created it to reduce the size of the population.'

'Are you being serious?' said Callum.

Grace turned in her sleeping bag. 'It's hit the west the hardest. Isn't that the poorest part of the country?'

The silence returned.

It was broken by Grace's tittering.

'That's not funny,' Louise said loud enough for them to all hear.

Grace burst out laughing, and others joined in. 'It's a conspiracy,' she yelled.

Callum sighed. 'I'm going to sleep now. Seun, Grace, if

you decide to get close while everyone's knocked out, keep the moaning and groaning to a minimum – please.'

Seun was glad it was dark as he couldn't see how embarrassed Grace was.

DAY 13

In the morning, Seun woke up to find that Louise was the first awake. She was telling everyone to get up. It was 5am, and the storm was less intense. No one spoke much, and before heading home Seun made sure he said bye to Grace, who responded with a tired smile as she rubbed her eyes.

'Get home safely,' she eventually said.

'I will.'

Seun said bye to everyone else and left the office.

At home, he tried to go back to sleep but couldn't. He received a message from Khensy: Hey, you alright?

I am.

Good. She continued: I'll be back as soon as the storm lets up. Promise.

He closed the conversation. He scrolled down until he reached the last message he had received from his dad. They had been talking about the outcome of a boxing match his father had watched, and it amused Seun when his dad went on to say that if he had continued fighting in his youth he would have gone on to be a threat like the sport had never seen.

What would your nickname have been? Seun had written.

The Unstoppable One, his father had replied, or something like that.

In the afternoon, Seun turned on the television in time for the weather forecast. It was the same weatherman, though he appeared drained; his tie was loose, and his white shirt had creases in it. He repeated that there would be no changes for the coming days and told everyone to stay safe. When the camera returned to the presenter, Seun noticed a hint of melancholy in her expression. She stuttered as she revealed that the confirmed death toll was now over three thousand, and she urged people to not head west, even if they had family and friends there. Seun checked his phone again. The last message from his dad was four days old. He stood up and got his coat, and when he opened the door, a burst of wind hit him. A chair was being blown down the road in front of his house and countless pieces of litter were airborne. Seun jumped back and slammed it shut. He stood still with his hands against the door window. His breathing became heavy, and after a few seconds he began thumping the door gently with his fist. His pounds became harder until he reeled back and punched it. The door shook, stinging his hand. Immediately, he started to kick it. His foot banged against the wood, and he yelled curses but couldn't hear his voice over the wind. When he was finally exhausted, he rested against the door until his knees ached from standing. He then dragged himself back and sat on a stair step. His phone beeped. It was from Grace.

I've been asleep since we came back from work.

There was a laughing face at the end of it. Seun closed the message. After several seconds he called his father's phone. It went to voicemail. He stared down at the space between his knees and only realised he was crying when he noticed the soft but bitter taste of his tears.

DAY 15

Along with Grace and Callum, Seun was having his dinner in the canteen. One of the cooks turned the volume of the television up as the weatherman came on, causing Seun to stop eating and to focus on the screen. He thought the weatherman now appeared distraught; he wore no tie and his shirt was too big for him. He wiped his forehead with a tissue, and when he lifted his arm Seun saw that the sweat patch beneath his armpit reached the rib area of his shirt. The studio had a grey tinge, but it lit up with a flash of lightning as the weatherman began to speak. The weatherman's eyes darted left for a moment, in the direction of the thunder, and then he began his report. He stopped only a few seconds in and glimpsed to his right. Someone was speaking to him. After some time, he returned his attention to the camera.

'Despite ... despite previous indications that the storm would fade this week, this now doesn't seem to be the case.' The weatherman fell silent. Everyone waited. He glanced away from the camera and towards the ground before looking back up. 'There is no end predicted to the storm.'

Instantly, confusion spread throughout the canteen. People started to mumble amongst themselves. Some, like Seun, kicked their seat back as they got up. The weatherman ended his forecast. Callum swore. Seun continued to stare at the TV, and when the camera returned to the main news report, he threw his bottle of drink at the screen, cracking it. Everyone stopped talking. They were now all watching him. Seun ignored them, staggering slightly as he picked up his stuff and made his way back to the office.

Louise peered out of her room, still sitting in her chair, as Seun entered and lifted his coat off the peg. 'What are you doing?'

'I'm heading west.'

'What on God's earth would make you want to go there? Have you not been watching the same news I have?'

Seun pulled his gloves on. 'My father's there. I haven't heard anything from him for six days now.' He zipped his coat up as the rest of the office workers came in. He stared at them. 'I'll be back tomorrow, hopefully.'

Callum eyed him. 'You're a brave fool.' He stepped forward and held Seun's shoulder. 'I should tell you not to, but you're stubborn, so, be safe, man. We'll see you tomorrow.'

Seun glanced at everyone else. He nodded once and then walked out.

When he heard footsteps behind him, he knew it was Grace. He turned around.

'How primitive are you?' Grace stopped when she was right in front of him. 'Running into danger when you know you shouldn't.'

Seun was quiet.

Grace shook her head. 'People do that, don't they? God knows why. But if I was you … I'd probably do the same.'

She rubbed underneath her nose and kept her fingers

there. She shut her eyes, and after a second she leaned forward and hugged him. 'Make sure you come back.'

Seun let go of her. 'Grace, Khensy—'

'Khensy's where?' Grace's eyes were wet, and she spoke quickly, almost harshly. 'Go on, where is she? Is she here now?'

'No. She isn't'

'Exactly … There's a name for people who we're attached to but who aren't actually here, you know?'

'What's that?'

'Imaginary friends.'

He laughed, and she smiled. When they locked eyes again, he leaned forward. He kissed her then pulled away. Grace still had her eyes closed. She licked her bottom lip slowly. Seun watched her, waiting for her to say something, and when she opened her eyes again he thought she was caught between joy and sadness. She turned around and headed back to the office. Seun waited until she was gone before continuing on his way out of the building.

From Crewchester to his father's house in Wrentpole was less than a two-hour drive, but Seun expected it to take longer, and as he approached the motorway, he felt himself beginning to sweat. There were no cars up ahead, and a message on the digital sign above the road showed a list of places that people were advised not to travel to. Wrentpole came up again and again. Seun expected to see an officer of some sort stationed at the motorway junction to turn people back, but there was nothing except a lamp post that had been blown over and which was now resting diagonally across the motorway. Upon seeing this, Seun wondered for the first time if the journey would kill him. His hands trembled on the steering wheel as the storm shrieked. Slowing down as he approached the fallen lamp post, he eased forward and went around it. He put pressure on the accelerator pedal, doubting his decision as he headed down the deserted motorway.

The trees on either side of the road were caught in an involuntary dance with the storm. At first, Seun saw no cars behind or ahead of him, but a few minutes into his drive he spotted one coming down on the other side of the motorway. He caught a glimpse of the driver. They were signalling with one hand for him to turn back. The car disappeared, and Seun focused on the road, trying not to think about the gesture. Soon after, he saw more vehicles heading in the direction opposite to him. The passengers in all of them stared at him as he passed. In one of them, he saw someone in the back seat frantically gesturing for him to turn around by waving their arms, making an X. Seun only caught this for a second, and when he looked forward again, he could hardly see the path in front of him due to the increasing rain.

The emptiness of the road meant he had enough room to progress without having to stay in one lane, and after an hour he slowed down and rested on the hard shoulder, waiting to see if the downpour would calm. It didn't. He snapped the radio on. Static. He switched stations, only to hear more of the same. He turned it off and continued forward.

The first time the wind was strong enough to cause him to lose control of his car, he stopped entirely. To feel his vehicle being thrown one direction, and to have the sight of his path turn into a twisted blur as the wheels disobeyed the commands he forced through the steering, made him shake, and he spent the moments after trying to control his shock. It took him time to regain his cool, but afterwards he continued onwards. Steadily at first, but as he was struck by the wind more and more often, he became used to the feeling of losing control and driving against the storm, but he was thankful for the empty lanes giving him the room to fight it. Over the next two hours, the storm intensified, forcing him to collide with the central reservation. He braked as the side of his car scraped alongside the concrete barrier and came to a halt. When he got out, the wind hit him, and he was slammed against the bonnet. He forced his way around the car and inspected the damage: the driver-side window had cracked, the left mirror had fallen off and there were scrapes and scratches along the side of the vehicle. His hood was blowing in front of his face, and he swore as he made his way back inside. He could smell blood and touched his lip; it was cut. It was getting darker, and the clouds were thick and heavy. The longer Seun gazed at them, the closer to the ground he thought they were. He saw a stroke of lightning, and others followed. Starting his car again, he set off, gradually increasing his speed. When he hit fifty miles-per-hour he kept on going, and when he reached seventy he pushed further on until he hit one hundred, going as fast as he could before the night caught him.

Seun drove like this for another hour. He slowed whenever he felt that the wind was going to throw him to the edge, but he always returned to the one hundred miles-per-hour mark.

When he left the motorway he expected the wind to reduce, but it felt just as violent.

The first thing Seun noticed when he reached Wrentpole was how much damage it had taken. Trees and lamp posts were embedded in buildings, doors were wide open, rubbish whirled through the air and streets were flooded. A pang of sadness hit him as he thought about the people who had been forced to leave their homes once warning of the storm arrived. As he went further, he tried to quell a troubling thought that had begun to develop in his mind, and as he headed towards his father's home the thought grew until he became more and more certain that it would be correct; that his dad had been killed by the storm.

The journey to his father's house after leaving the motorway should have taken him less than fifteen minutes, but after thirty, Seun was still navigating pools of water and waste. During this time, he was grateful for the storm's ability to focus his attention. He glanced up as he drove and saw gashes of lightning scarring the clouds as the storm disturbed the approaching night. What had once been broken roars was now a constant, resonant sound, and Seun was unable to think of anything else but the violent nature around him. His car was hit by several small pieces of flying debris, causing his windscreen to crack.

It took him another half hour to reach the street his father lived on. Once there, he could make out the house, and he saw the balcony was still intact and that the lamp posts were still standing. As he neared it, he saw that the tree beside his father's home had been uprooted and thrown into the right side of it. Seun accelerated. He braked hard once he was in the middle of the road opposite the house, and he climbed out so quickly that he forgot about the wind and was blown over. He struggled to his feet and ran to the front door. It was still locked. He pulled his hood down to stop it blowing into his face and searched around. The damage done to the house meant he could climb into it without bothering with the door, but, wanting to hold onto some normality, he took out the key he kept to his father's home and unlocked it. Inside was pitch-black. He tried the light switch. It didn't work, so he used the torch on his phone – expecting it to reveal havoc, but the passageway appeared untouched. For a moment, Seun was about to shout his dad's name, but knowing the storm had broken into the house created a new terror in him; it owned the house now, and he felt the need to remain quiet so as to not offend it. Instead, he decided to concentrate on finding a body.

He climbed upstairs. The house smelled damp, and he could hear water dripping. He lifted his torch as he went down the corridor towards his father's bedroom and jumped back when the light shone onto the trunk of the tree. Seun aimed the torch upwards; there was a hole where the tree had torn into the house, and through it he could see lightning chasing itself while the faint moon watched. His phone vibrated. He ignored it. The tree stopped him from going any further. Seun retreated, not taking his eyes off the ruin in front of him until he reached the stairs. He wheeled around and descended into the living room, which was below his father's bedroom and next to the garden. There, the fallen tree took up most of the space, and the litter-filled wind was blowing stronger, forcing Seun to shield his face. He advanced, pointing the torch around the trunk, and saw scattered pieces of wardrobe along with crushed plaster and brick. There were thick branches in his way, and he pushed them aside. The light passed a red wound on the wood. Seun shone it back on the area. His pulse quickened. It was blood. He scanned further and stopped when he discovered what looked like bits of his father's pyjamas. They were stained scarlet and covered in twigs. He hurried onto his hands and knees and cast the torchlight around until he found something. The light rested on a twisted leg. The sight made him spin round, and he hit a branch with his face as he did. He snapped it with his free hand and stumbled out of the living room into the passageway. He rested one of his hands on a radiator and wanted to stop himself from trembling but couldn't. Letting go, he slid down the wall beside it until he was resting on the floor. The urge to sob came over him, and he tried to fight it, but when he remembered it was just him and the storm, he let it out.

Seun remained there, sitting and wiping his tears in the cold of the passageway until he fell asleep.

DAY 16

When Seun woke, he could tell it was past midnight by how cold it had become. He pushed himself up before checking his phone. It was still on, and there were two messages from Khensy. He rubbed his eyes as he made his way to the staircase.

The first message read: I tried to call you, but it's not

getting through. I'm guessing you've seen the news. Ring me when you can.

Seun felt his swollen lip and stared up at the stairs. And as he began to climb them, he read Khensy's second message: Hopefully they're wrong and this storm disappears soon 'cause I want to see you. Love you.

Seun peered ahead and tried to orient himself in the darkness. He lifted his phone's torch; he was facing the direction that led to the balcony. He headed towards it. When he reached the cracked, double glass doors he paused. He listened to the storm and thought about what Khensy's message had said and for how much longer he would be unable to see her. He typed a reply.

What if they're not wrong?

After he sent it, he received a notification telling him the message had failed to deliver. He looked through the glass; his father's chair had been blown towards the end of the balcony balustrade. Glaring up at the storm, he pulled one of the doors open and stepped outside. The wind pushed him back. He turned his back on it and lifted the chair, positioning it so that it was resting against the end of the balcony, so that when he sat down, he was facing the storm. Seun turned the torch on his phone off. He was tense, and around him the sound of thunder clapped again and again. After some moments he calmed, and he became thankful to the boom of the wind and its rattling rain for not allowing him enough time to concentrate and to think about his dad. His phone vibrated. It was a message from Grace.

Are you okay?

He replied: No, I'm not, but thank you for asking. He

expected the message to not deliver, but it did. He smiled a bit.

Seun was tempted to glance at the destruction of the house, but he gritted his teeth and resisted the urge so as to not refuel the pain he was already feeling. He kept his eyes on the turmoil of the sky and allowed himself to become fully captivated by it without any interruptions and without fighting back.

Eden

When Fia breathed in the air around Eden's hotel, she was certain it had been laced with a fragrance. She gazed at the building's structure; it resembled several mansions joined together and was partly hidden by tall trees. As she wandered, she expected to feel raindrops on her skin the way they would at home, but here the air was still, and the few clouds present were vibrant.

A man and a woman in green and white uniforms were on either side of the hotel entrance. Once she reached them, the woman said, 'Welcome to Eden.'

Fia smiled. She stepped forward, pulling her suitcase behind her, and advanced inwards then towards the front desk where another man was seated. He greeted her. She handed her passport to him, and he pushed it into an electronic slot beneath the desk before giving it back to her.

'Take a seat through the double doors, and someone will come out to see you.'

Fia thanked him. She headed towards the doors and they opened automatically, revealing a long, wide corridor with several chairs opposite a row of meeting rooms. The smell was pleasant, like outside, but fainter. Fia took a seat and studied the polished surfaces of the spacious surroundings. After a few moments, a tall woman in a green and white outfit came out of one of the rooms. The woman was carrying a tablet, and she glanced at it before looking up. 'Fia?'

Fia got up and the woman gestured for her to come in.

Inside, Fia sat behind a circular table and inspected the room. There were large windows at the back, but the view was mostly blocked by branches and leaves, making the room dimmer than the waiting area.

'How was your flight?'

'Good.'

The woman took her seat, which was at the other end of the table and by a computer. 'I think I remember you. You came with your family last year.'

Fia glanced away and stared down at her hands. 'I did.'

'You've probably forgotten; my name's Jasmine. Feel free to ask me any questions, and once I've checked your details, I'll give you the key to your room.'

Jasmine explained to Fia what benefits she could make use of during her stay, as well as the hotel's regulations, and how she would be helped both inside and outside the hotel if necessary. Once she had finished talking, Jasmine put a welcome pack and a key on the table.

'Who are you hoping to see?' Jasmine asked, focusing on her screen.

Fia hesitated. She glanced at the wall and noticed the slight movement of the shadows that the branches outside cast.

'It's alright,' Jasmine added. 'You don't have to tell me.'

'I want to see my brother.'

Jasmine glimpsed from her monitor to Fia. 'Okay … I know you already know, but I have to stress that the likelihood of him appearing again is extremely low.'

'I know.' Fia concentrated on Jasmine's outfit to avoid meeting her eyes.

Jasmine reached down and opened a drawer. She pulled out a leaflet bearing the title Bereavement Counselling.

'No.'

'Just consider it, Fia. I think—'

Fia pushed her chair back and stood up. 'No. I'm fine.'

Jasmine laid the leaflet on the table between them. She handed Fia the welcome pack and the key.

'Everything I've told you and all that you'll need during your stay is in the pack. Your room number's on the key also.'

Fia took the items from her.

'I hope you have a lovely time here, and I hope that you see your brother.'

'Me too.'

Jasmine put her hand forward.

Fia shook it. 'Thank you.'

She turned around slowly to avoid appearing eager to leave but couldn't hide the slightly hurried pace in which she exited.

Her room was large, and like the meeting room, the view through its windows was interrupted by tree limbs and petals. It was silent, save for the faint sound of footsteps passing her door from time to time and the low song of the wind. She unpacked. Afterwards, as she was lying in her bed staring at the ceiling, she heard steps outside again, but this time they were accompanied by someone talking. She slipped off her bed and padded towards her door. The steps became harder to hear and eventually faded. Fia opened her door and leaned out. She looked from one end of the curving passageway to the other and saw no one. Sticking out further, she heard the footsteps returning, and a man appeared at the end of the corridor who was staring down as he paced with his arms folded. She heard him whisper to himself and sigh. He raised his head and noticed her. Fia gave a smile that she thought must have seemed forced and awkward.

'I didn't think anyone else was here,' the man said as he neared her. 'God, I must look like a lunatic walking back and forth like this.'

'It's fine. I didn't think I'd meet anyone else while I was here either.' Fia eyed the ceiling and the walls. 'It's so big.'

The man smiled. He had a beard and appeared to be in his forties, but he looked tired, which made him seem older. 'Same. It's nice to speak to someone too. Are you here with family?'

Fia shook her head.

'Me neither.' The man glanced around the corridor and at the intricate patterns on the wallpaper. 'This place, this whole structure, it's incredible.'

'Yeah, it is. The garden too.'

The man's eyes widened. 'You've been already? How come you're still here?'

'No, I've been in the past – with my family.' Fia watched his expression change.

'So this is your second time?' The man shook his head. 'I'm sorry for your losses – physical and financial.'

'Thanks … It's been hard.'

'When did you arrive?'

'A few hours ago. You?'

'Yesterday. Or the day before. I'm not sure now. You lose track in this place. I'm in room six twenty-six.' He pointed behind him. 'A few doors down.'

'You still haven't been yet?'

'No … It's not easy.'

'I know.'

The man peered down at the carpet and put his hands in his pockets. Fia was about to change the subject when he continued.

'It's my mum I'm here to see. She died years ago – before the storm and all, but I never went with my family the first time.'

'Oh.'

'Sorry. I'm being weird talking about this, aren't I?'

'If there's a place where it's okay to tell a stranger about your deceased loved ones, it's here.'

The man laughed loudly. 'My God.' He wiped his eyes. 'That's true.'

Fia left her doorway and searched from one end of the corridor to the other. They were the only people there. 'What's stopping you going down?'

'I never got on with her – my mum. That's why I didn't go the first time, but it's troubled my conscience ever since. So, I saved up the money, and here I am.' He twiddled his beard. 'If she appears, I don't know what I'm going to say to her.' He looked up at the ceiling. 'Flipping hell,' he said, still staring upwards, 'I'm glad she's gone.'

Fia cleared her throat.

'Sorry.'

'It's okay. Don't be.'

The man took his hands out of his pockets. 'Who are you here to see?'

Fia thought about her brother, Sam. She remembered his rude sense of humour along with his cheeky, constant criticisms and the face he used to pull whenever she'd do something silly. 'I'm here to see my older brother again. Well, I'm hoping to. He passed four years ago tomorrow.'

'Because of the storm?'

She nodded.

'I'm sorry. I hope you see him.'

'Yeah.' She bit her lip. 'When will you go to the garden?'

'Not sure,' the man said. 'I'm a bit scared. What if she looks and smells … undead?'

'She won't. I understand, though. It's a lot to take in.'

'It is.' The man fell silent for a moment. 'Sod it, I'll go now. By the time you wake up after going to bed, I'll be gone.'

'I hope you see her.'

The man nodded. 'Me too. And thanks.'

Fia watched him walk away before re-entering her room.

She woke up several hours later to the glare of the sun blinking between the trees and through the open blinds. Her nose tickled, and her room smelled of the same scented air of the grounds. The fragrance pleased her. She spent several minutes in her bed, breathing it in, and found that she felt happier, and that her sensitivity to the colours around her was enhanced. When she focused her gaze on the leaves of the trees outside, they became a vibrant wall of colour capable of showing a face or an abstract expression when they moved in the wind. She stared, and the colours thickened; she was no longer seeing a tree but a steady waterfall of images that was detailed enough for her to see the ridges of paint that the brush of scent had left. She didn't know how much time had passed before she finally sat up. She surveyed her room before opening her window, and she had to blink repeatedly for the hues in front of her to become less intense. She came away from the window and took a photo of her and Sam from her suitcase before resting on her bed again. She studied it. In the picture, she was grinning straight into the camera. She shut her eyes as she lay down and tried to keep hold of the image in her mind as she allowed herself to fall asleep again.

The glow from Fia's window hadn't receded when she woke up. After she had dressed, she examined herself in the mirror and tried to see if there were any signs of tiredness etched onto her face. She assessed herself from different angles, gauging how much she had aged since the last time she had seen her brother. Her hair was the same as it was in the photo, but she thought her smile was thinner. She left her room and made her way down the corridor. As she neared room six twenty-six, she could hear the man inside, still moving about and mumbling to himself. The noise stopped as she came closer. Fia chuckled quietly and walked on while following the signs that led to the garden. She passed the lift and went down a spiral staircase, then through a long, spacious corridor with ceilings at such a height that she wondered at the effort that must have gone into the building's construction. She continued for several minutes until she could see a strong light coming from a large archway. When she got closer, she saw a man and a woman in the distinctive green and white of the Eden uniform standing either side of it. They smiled at her. Fia peered into the garden ahead and could hear water as well as a soft breeze. Her heart started to race when she stepped onto the stone path of the garden and breathed in the fragrant air. She closed her eyes as she felt the warmth of Eden surround her.

Fia gazed up at the trees, noticing that many of the smaller ones bore fruit. Her nervousness left her with barely any appetite so she pulled down only a couple of grapes. She washed them in a low stream first, of which there were many, despite being sure that there was no need to. It was warm but not uncomfortably so, and she had lost track of how long she had been walking. There were clear paths between the bushes throughout the garden no matter which route she took. She was sure that it was changing to suit her wherever she went, and she had been trying to lose herself in order to find herself in an area where the path was absent, but after several attempts she had given up. Now, she followed a stream that was clear enough for her to see the earth beneath it, but she could see no fish, and she realised then she had seen no other form of life since she had entered the garden. She rested on a curved rock and took her shoes off. In front of her, past the stream, there were groups of tall flowers amongst neatly shaped bushes, making Fia wonder if the staff she had seen maintained the garden. She took the photo of her and Sam out of her pocket. Despite it snowing in the picture, Fia thought he was wearing too much, yet his woolly hat was only halfway on and revealed the front of his braided hair. He was looking away from the camera, smirking at something else.

'Sam,' she whispered, 'I know you're angry at me for spending so much and coming here again. I know you'd rather I'd saved it, but I'm—' Fia heard the sound of something moving and spun around.

'You know talking to yourself is the first sign of madness?'

Fia covered her mouth in shock. His hair was still braided like it was in the photo, and his face hadn't changed.

'You haven't aged well at all,' Sam said. 'Maybe you should come and join me sooner.' He laughed while coming forward.

'I didn't think you'd come.' Fia felt his arms wrap around her.

'I wasn't going to ... You shouldn't be here.'

'I know.' She kept her face in the middle of his chest.

'You need to move on. Everyone else has. Not to mention how much these bastards are charging ... This is a luxury, Fia. How many people wish they could afford to come here, just once, to see their relatives-turned-zombies?'

She leaned back and punched his shoulder. 'You're not a zombie.' She pressed her forehead onto his collar bone. 'I'm sorry for coming, but I've got no one else.'

'Shut up. You do. You have a great life. Don't spend it on the dead.'

Fia bit her bottom lip as her eyes started to water, and she felt Sam gently trying to push her off him.

'God,' he said, 'a whole year since I saw you last and you haven't changed your hair in the slightest.'

'I will.'

'How's home? And the storm?'

Fia shook her head. 'Better, but not much.'

Sam was quiet. 'Aren't you going to ask how I've been?'

'How have you been?'

'That's a stupid question. I've been dead.'

Fia rolled her eyes.

'All jokes aside, if you come again, I won't show up. I mean it. I won't come down. I'll stay up there, watching you walk around like an idiot.'

Fia chuckled under her breath. 'Okay.'

'And that goes for everyone else who loves me enough to spend thousands to come and see me.'

Fia ignored his comment. She placed her ear against her brother's chest and imagined his heart beating above the sound of the stream and beneath the ripple of the wind as it brushed the trees overhead.

Seize

Omar woke up at 5:30am. He ate a bowl of cereal while standing up. After he had finished, he opened his windows and sat on his bed in his boxers. He rolled a spliff, smoked it, then went back to sleep. When he woke again, it was 8:30 am. Once he had a shower, he put on some music and got dressed. He put a change of clothes into a rucksack and tidied up after himself then set his phone to silent and slipped it into his top cabinet drawer along with his ID. He opened the compartment below and took out a small bag of cocaine, which he half emptied in a line onto his table before pressing his finger on his right nostril, closing it, and sniffing the line with his left. Omar shut his eyes and breathed in. He felt his body warm and his heart pound. He returned what was left then grabbed his motorcycle helmet and rucksack.

He left his flat and made his way to his bike.

A road light turned amber. Omar stopped, and people crossed. He was sweating, and he bit his bottom lip while the sound of rain needled its way through his helmet. The cracking noise it caused failed to break his focus, and he tried to remain calm despite feeling impatient at the amount of time the lights were taking to change. When the light turned green, he edged forward. He could feel his heart pumping.

Everything was enhanced; the streets felt busier, the wet weather tested his reflexes more and he had a greater awareness of the cars beside him. He clenched the handlebars of his bike and sped onto the pavement towards the jeweller's. Before he could ask himself where his partners were, he saw Conor and Alfie appear from the opposite direction, one after the other, riding onto the pathway outside the shop. Confusion quickly turned into panic when the bikes came into view. The people on the footpath dispersed, but most continued to watch once they were at a far enough distance. The quaking engines of the other motorcycles calmed Omar. He swung his bike round so that he was facing the entrance to the jeweller's. Yanking his front wheel up, he accelerated forward and burst through the doors. Behind him, Alfie stayed on his bike outside the shop and started burning out his motorcycle. Omar could hear the commotion, and when he glanced back over his shoulder, he saw Alfie peering in all directions as the smoke from his wheel spread and began to cloud the view. Conor ran inside to join him. He raised four fingers, showing Omar how many minutes they had, then pulled an axe out of his bag, causing those on the shop floor to scatter. Omar ignored the frightened customers, who began to flee or huddle in groups. He whipped his sledge-hammer out and saw Conor indicate which cabinets to break open.

Omar smashed a cupboard apart. Most of the staff were running for cover or hiding in a corner. He grabbed several watches then continued to the next.

After a few minutes, he saw Conor glance at his watch then signal for them to make an exit, and they both ran towards the door. The noise of Alfie's bike was reassuring. There were no sirens, only the sound of the motorcycle revving. Omar jumped onto his bike and rushed out of the shop and onto the road. The rubber of the handlebars dug into his gloves, and he tried to ease the tightening of his biceps and the locking of his elbows but couldn't. He glanced back once to see Alfie and Conor heading in separate directions. He manoeuvred through traffic, unable to relax until he was miles away from the jeweller's and the pedestrians around him weren't aware that a robbery had taken place.

Through the window of his flat, Omar saw two kids cycling in circles around a puddle. They were in shorts, despite the wind that was nudging the antennas on houses and the rain that was cascading in streams off the corners of large bins. His phone vibrated, showing a message from his sister, Marai.

When are you planning to visit? Lucee keeps asking. She wants to see her uncle.

He replied: Whenever I'm free and whenever the weather isn't so bad.

Omar clutched his phone; an unwanted thought of how his niece would perceive him if she was ever told how her uncle made a living entered his mind. It lingered. He chucked his phone onto his bed and stood still with his hands in his pockets. He gazed out of his window and waited for the thought to fade.

Outside the barbershop, Grant coughed after toking on a cigarette. He cleared his throat. 'How'd it go?'

Omar observed him from underneath his hood. 'You weren't there.'

'I know… I'm going to be a dad. I'm not focused on anything else at the moment. And you have to be when you're out there.'

Omar watched Grant disappear under his umbrella as he went to put his cigarette out on top of a bin.

'We've settled on a name for him,' Grant said as he reappeared.

'What you calling him?'

'Omar.'

Omar leaned back and stared at Grant. Grant grinned, and Omar laughed hard.

'It's a cautious name, man. We want him to be like that: cool, calm and collected.'

Smiling, Omar patted Grant on the back. 'He's going to be a rider.'

Grant chuckled. 'We're not naming him after you. You just happen to have the same name as him.'

'It's like that, yeah?'

'It is.'

'You riding next time?'

Grant scratched his nose. 'Not sure.'

Omar watched his friend sift through his pockets until he found his pack of cigarettes. He lifted the lid and started to pull one out. He stopped when it was a quarter-way out of the box.

'I need to quit.' Grant put the packet back in his pocket and stared across the road in silence.

On the day of the next raid, Omar woke at 6am. He had a bowl of cereal, standing up, and once he'd finished, he opened his windows then sat on his bed. He rolled a spliff, smoked it then went back to sleep. When he woke up, it was 9am. He had a shower and got dressed. Afterwards, he put a change of clothes into his rucksack. When it was 10:30am, he pulled open the middle drawer and took out the bag of cocaine. He snorted a line. He left his phone and wallet in the top drawer, before picking up his motorcycle helmet and rucksack and leaving the house.

As Omar broke open a cabinet, Conor aimed his axe at some of the jeweller's staff who were inching towards them. Omar tightened his bag. He checked outside and saw people turning away from the jeweller's and parting as if to make way for something approaching from the end of the road. He made the sign for police, and once he was sure that Conor had seen it, he ran to the exit. Alfie was waiting outside the shop, and as Omar sprinted he saw Conor, who was dashing towards his bike, get tackled to the ground by a larger man. Without hesitation, Alfie swung his sledgehammer into the attacker, causing him to hit the ground and roll. Alfie then mounted his motorcycle while Conor struggled upwards and clambered on to his own. Omar noticed the police cars in the distance fighting to get through the traffic. Once Alfie and Conor had started to move, he slipped onto his bike. He rode off the pavement onto the road and broke away from the few bystanders who were brave enough to jump at him. He looked back and slowed to a halt when he saw Conor wrestling with more assailants. Further down the street he spotted a police car approaching and people pointing in their direction. He snapped his head to the side as he felt something pull at him; a woman was shouting, trying to prise him off his bike by grabbing his bag of stolen watches. He shoved her, and she pulled harder. The longer he struggled the more he noticed others nearby advancing towards him and beginning to encircle him. He headbutted her, causing her to stumble to the ground, then heard yelling and felt someone hook his arm with theirs and heave him off his motorcycle. He almost fell on his side but stopped himself by spinning round, and as he did so he swung his sledgehammer at the two men in front of him. He hit one of them in the stomach, making them crumple and hold where the hammer had collided. The other stopped advancing in order to help the one Omar had injured. Omar climbed back onto his bike and accelerated without registering the grunts of pain coming from those he had hurt. He was breathing heavily, and he felt his body ache. He glimpsed back for a second and saw the same people who had been encircling him gathering watches off the ground. He checked his bag. It was open. Further along the street, Conor and Alfie were trying to escape the police who were surrounding them. Omar re-sealed his bag and swung it to his front as he swerved through traffic.

He spent several minutes trying to find an alleyway that

wasn't frequented by homeless people. When he did, he dipped into it, got off his bike and abandoned it there. He entered a pub and headed to the toilets. In one of the cubicles he changed into the clothes that he had in his rucksack and put what he was wearing before in a plastic bag. He was careful not to draw attention to himself as he left and apologised to two people who he bumped into upon exiting. He found a large bin, belonging to a restaurant that wasn't open yet, and threw the bag into it.

At home, he withheld his number and rang Conor. There was no answer. He tried Alfie. No answer.

He didn't move. It was noisy from the kids outside riding their bikes as well as the music from the floor below him. He shut his window. He gathered his ID and personal documents then put some clothes, cash and a few other items in a large suitcase and left.

Omar dropped a few coins into the slot of a payphone and entered Marai's number. He watched people walk past, and whenever someone came near, he glanced at his suitcase, which was outside, resting beside the telephone box. Marai's phone continued to ring and Omar closed his eyes as he waited for her to answer.

'Hello?' Marai said.

'It's Omar.'

'Where are you calling from?'

'A phone box. How's Lucee?'

'... She's good.'

Omar stared at the ground. He put his forearm under his

nose to give him a moment's relief from the smell of piss. 'I'm coming to Holmechester tonight.'

'What? Tonight? Are you sure you don't want to wait and see if the weather calms? It's not good at the minute. I know it's not bad compared to other places, but you're better off in Denttingham right now, trust me.'

'Marai, I don't have a choice.'

Marai fell silent. She sighed. 'Okay. Lucee will be happy anyway... Are you on your way?'

'Not yet. In an hour or two.'

'How long are you staying for?'

Omar rubbed his eyes and looked out at the night. Several people were skulking in the darkness of the street, and he could hear the noise of the city. He felt exposed. He spoke into the phone in a low voice, 'A while.'

No answer.

'Hello?'

'How are you for money?'

'I'm good.'

Omar heard Lucee's excited chattering in the background.

'Tell me when you're here.'

'I will.'

Before Omar had a chance to say thank you, Marai hung up.

'Where to?' the driver shouted over the rain that had started to fall.

Omar climbed into the taxi. 'Train station.' When the car

began turning, he leaned forward. 'Go to the newsagent's first.'

The driver nodded in the mirror.

In the shop, Omar bought a pen and a card that said *New Baby Boy*. He hurried back to the taxi. 'Go to this address.'

He glimpsed out of the window as the taxi approached Grant's house. He carefully wrote a message in the card before opening the door and asking the driver to wait. Small stones crunched underneath his feet as he walked along the path. Grant's front garden was neat, and the kitchen lights were on. Omar thought about the prospects of a child running around inside the house who also shared his name, and it raised his spirits a little as he lifted the letterbox and pushed the card through. As he returned to the taxi, he glanced back at Grant's house. Knowing it would likely be the last time he would see it caused his emotions to harden again.

'Someone important?' the driver asked as Omar opened the taxi door.

Omar didn't answer. 'To the station.'

The driver didn't speak again and turned the radio on before moving.

Omar didn't look back.

Marc Populaire

TUESDAY, DECEMBER 28TH, 1999

09:03 *You've reached Marc. Leave a message.*
Hey Marc, it's John. I came round to have a look at the boiler, but no one was in. I can come again the same time tomorrow. Let me know.

12:26 *You've reached Marc. Leave a message.*
It's you-know-who. Call me back.

15:49 *You've reached Marc. Leave a message.*
It's John again. Sorry, I can't do tomorrow, but I can do Friday. To be honest, Marc, your boiler probably only needs a quick adjustment. Don't let all this talk about freak storms brewing cook you into a panic. They've been saying that every year for the past thirty years. I'm sure what you need can wait until the new year. Let me know if Friday's good for you anyway. Cheers.

19:48 *You've reached Marc. Leave a message.*
Marc, it's your father. I don't know why you're ignoring my calls. Have things got worse? If you need help, call me. Don't be stubborn.

21:30 *You've reached Marc. Leave a message.*
It's me again. I bumped into Thomas and Tessa today. I told them you've applied for bankruptcy.

Don't get mad. They would've found out anyway. Give me a ring. I need to know when you're moving in.

22:01 *You've reached Marc. Leave a message.*
Hey, it's Rebecca. I thought I'd ring you, seeing as it's been days and you still haven't called me. Ring me when you can ... Love you.

23:47 *You've reached Marc. Leave a message.*
It's Sharm. I'm assuming you don't want to speak to me, seeing as you haven't been answering my calls the past few days, but ... shouldn't I be the one ignoring you? Have you forgotten whose fault this all is? Forget it. I wasn't calling to argue. I just wanted to let you know how the kids were. I'm not expecting you to call back.

WEDNESDAY, DECEMBER 29TH, 1999

11:14 *You've reached Marc. Leave a message.*
Hey, what's up? It's Thomas. Tessa and I bumped into Roshane yesterday. It was good to see him, but you know him, he can talk non-stop. Anyway, he told us about your situation ... Sorry to hear. If I can help in any way let me know. And remember, Marc, the bad times are only bad when you're going through them.

16:47 *You've reached Marc. Leave a message.*
Hi Dad ... Sanya's got a boyfriend. He's like ten times older than her, and he's got a beard, and—

What the hell, Ray?! Give me the phone. Now! Dad,
I haven't got a boyfriend. Ray's chatting shit – sorry.
Bye, Dad. Ray, you little—!

17:09 *You've reached Marc. Leave a message.*
Hi Dad, sorry about my last message. Are we seeing
you on New Year's Eve?... Sanya's lying, Dad.
She's seeing someone. He looks about fifty, and—
Ray!

17:21 *You've reached Marc. Leave a message.*
Marc Populaire ... What's happening? It's Uzair.
Long time no speak. Let me cut to it: on New Year's
Eve I'm finally opening that club I always talked
about. I know right? About time. Anyway, I want
you to be involved. I know you've got your own
thing going on, but let me talk to you about it.
Call me back.

18:30 *You've reached Marc. Leave a message.*
What you doing? How come you're not answering?
I've left two messages. Call me.

20:07 *You've reached Marc. Leave a message.*
It's Sharm. Ray and Sanya were being silly. Sanya
has got a boyfriend. She's had one for a while.
I've sorted it ... This is how it starts, you know?
Depression, and things like that. You're going to
lose everything now, no matter what, and locking
yourself away isn't going to help... and that doesn't
trouble me. You don't deserve support. You don't
even deserve a second chance, but, despite
everything, I still care enough to not want to see
you in ruins. Anyway, bye.

20:41　*You've reached Marc. Leave a message.*
Marc? Are you there? Stop ignoring me and your
father. Your brother called and said you've been
ignoring him too. Are you okay? I don't want to
speak to this machine. Call me back.

THURSDAY, DECEMBER 30TH, 1999

08:12　*You've reached Marc. Leave a message.*
Hi, it's Rebecca. Just checking if you got my message
… Have you told Sharm about us? Is that what's
going on? Or are you hiding from something?
Whatever it is, you can tell me. I don't care what it is,
just call me, please.

12:13　*You've reached Marc. Leave a message.*
It's Uzair. I called Roshane after you didn't get back
to me. You know I'm impatient. He told me what's
happened… My offer's open, man. Take it. You're
losing your house here. I'm your only hope right
now. Think: a club won't go out of business the same
way a little menswear shop will. Music and drinks
don't go out of fashion, and people always want a
little bit extra on a night out … That's how you gain
extra financial security – not by playing by the rules;
that's how you go bankrupt. Call me.

17:30　*You've reached Marc. Leave a message.*
Hello? For God's sake call me back.

19:25　*You've reached Marc. Leave a message.*
It's Uzair. I missed your call but got your voicemail.

Smart move. We'll meet in the new year. No, in fact, come to the club tomorrow. Give me a call and we'll arrange a time.

21:51 *You've reached Marc. Leave a message.*

It's me, Sharm. I'm assuming you're hearing this but ignoring me because I didn't let you see the kids this Christmas. Listen closely, Marc; Sanya and Ray didn't get presents this year. That's because of you. That holiday we promised them isn't happening any more, because of you. Ray's not getting that new Game Boy, because of you. Sanya's not getting a new bike, because of you, and to top it off we're staying in this tiny apartment on the edge of a shithole, because of you. But do you know what really vexes me? You're acting like you're the one who's suffered the most.

21:57 *You've reached Marc. Leave a message.*

You understand why I'm not letting you see them right now, don't you? You don't tell your family you're going to be able to fix everything when you can't. You don't start fucking some other woman because you're stressed. You don't push and shove the mother of your children when she confronts you about it. You don't do that, Marc, you don't, and now you're paying for it ... I don't know how long you're going to ignore me, and I don't care, but I'm not going to be the one that stops speaking, and that's only because of Ray and Sanya, but ... This is stressing me out. Your silence, the bankruptcy, the kids ... Rebecca ... God, I think I've drunk too

63

much. Do you still see her? After everything that's happened. Are you with her now? Are you having fun? Forget it… No matter how much I think about it, it doesn't make sense … but you weren't happy, so maybe there's sense in what you did, because that's what people do when they're unhappy, right?

22:30 *You've reached Marc. Leave a message.*

Seriously? This is my fifth voicemail now. Call me back … You know what? Don't. Call me when you're ready to face your problems. You always do this. Every time you get into trouble, you hide. Don't get me wrong, I know it's been a hard couple months, but there's still some positives: you've got your health, your sanity, and Sharm will come round, believe me, even if she was harsh about Christmas. You just need to grovel … Listen to what I'm saying: it isn't as bad you think. You can start from scratch. So what if Marc Populaire takes a back seat while regular Marc gets himself together? What matters is how you bounce back. Call me.

22:37 *You've reached Marc. Leave a message.*

Also, Uzair rang me. Don't even think about getting mixed up with him. He's a good friend, but I wouldn't change my money with him. That reminds me, Tessa and Thomas are celebrating their wedding anniversary soon. There's going to be a ton of people. We can check that out and maybe it will take your mind off things. You need it.

07:33 *You've reached Marc. Leave a message.*
Hi Dad, it's Sanya… Mum's been drinking again.
She's been up late sitting by the kitchen counter and
leaving you messages. She's leaving empty bottles in
the bin. She's not even trying to hide it. Every day
she tells us how useless you are, but why does she
keep ringing you then? I don't—
Sanya, who are you talking to?
No one.
Get off the phone.
Mum—
Now!

09:24 *You've reached Marc. Leave a message.*
It's Roshane. I'm spending New Year's Eve with Mum
and Dad. You need to spend it with Sharm and the
kids. Call her.
And if you don't call me by tomorrow, I'm coming
round. Happy New Year.

10:17 *You've reached Marc. Leave a message.*
It's Rebecca. I know, I've rung you a few times, but
it's New Year's Eve, and I have to call everyone and
wish them well. That includes you, so… Happy New
Year, Marc.

11:35 *You've reached Marc. Leave a message.*
Hey, it's Thomas—
And Tessa!
We're just calling to give you a slightly early Happy
New Year message. We hope you're doing well and

that you're keeping your head up. Roshane said he
was going to tell you about our wedding—
Make sure you come, Marc.
Yes, make sure you do. It's in February.
We'll send you an invitation card.
We will. Take care—
And say hello to Sharm and the kids for me.
Tessa! He's—
Shit, I forgot. Quick, put the phone—

12:01   You've reached Marc. Leave a message.
It's Uzair. Are you coming tonight? Let me know.

12:33   *You've reached Marc. Leave a message.*
Marc, it's your mother. Happy New Year. We hope
you are alright. We're not worried too much because
we know what you're like, but it'd be good if you
called us, just to put our minds at rest. God bless,
Marc. We love you.

13:01   *You've reached Marc. Leave a message.*
It's Sharm. I know Sanya was talking to you earlier.
I don't know what she said, but I'm fine. The
apartment hasn't got much room, but we're good.
We're happy. Just thought I'd let you know. Bye.

14:14   *You've reached Marc. Leave a message.*
Marc? Are you coming? Let me know. It's Uzair.

15:51   *You've reached Marc. Leave a message.*
It's Sharm. I don't even know why I'm calling…
Bloody Sanya. She's as stubborn as you. She's
been arguing with me because you're not here.
It's annoying… How's your New Year's Eve going?

18:22   *You've reached Marc. Leave a message.*
It's Uzair. If you're coming, I'll see you at the club, but I'm taking your failure to call me back as you saying you're no longer interested.

19:33   *You've reached Marc. Leave a message.*
Marc, sometimes, I hate you. I want to hurt you – you and Rebecca – but then sometimes… I want you here. I don't understand it. Why did you do this to us? Your own family. You're— Ray, get out.
Mum? Are you okay?

20:41   *You've reached Marc. Leave a message.*
Dad, it's Sanya. I've been fighting Mum all day. Ray won't leave our room – we're sharing a room, Dad, and we're in crappy flat on the edge of Wrentpole right by the slums. Mum won't even tell us what's happening. Why are we here? How come we're not at home? I—
Mum, Sanya, Dad's outside. He's at the door. Can I open it?
He's what? No.
Open it.
Sanya, be quiet. Ray—
Open the door, Ray.
I'm opening it.
Don't you—!
Mum, please!
Sanya, no… No
Please…
No, I won't… Just… Let him in.

67

MONDAY, JANUARY 3RD, 2000

09:43 *You've reached Marc. Leave a message.*
It's John. Do you still want me to check your boiler?

Benjamin's Mansion

The mansion foyer was filled with voices and smelled of clean, cold air from outside layered with cologne and perfume. Moses, Julian and Evan were leaning beside the wall leading to the entrance of the living room in the midst of a crowd that was growing in number, and they watched as cheerful new arrivals were already behaving as if they were the only ones there.

Moses unfolded his arms and pulled from his jacket pocket the invitation card he had received from the party's host, Benjamin. He put his glasses on and read it:

> I was going to write a formal invitation, Moses, but it's you, so I'll write whatever. I'm having a party at the mansion – celebrating for the sake of celebrating. Bring Julian and Evan as I don't think they've been before. Strangers are welcome too, but make sure they're not too crazy.
>
> There's something special in one of the rooms I want someone to find. Whoever discovers it first can take anything from the mansion home with them, but they have to find it before midnight – can't make it too easy. Let your friends know.
>
> *Benjamin & Krista Kind*

'C'mon.' Moses pushed away from the wall, and Julian joined him. 'I'm going to search for whatever it is Benjamin's hidden.'

'I'm not feeling it,' said Evan.

Moses came to a halt. 'I'm not having that; save the insecurities for another day. I didn't get invited and come all this way just to stand around feeling awkward.'

Along with Julian, Moses started towards the main bar, but he stopped when he realised Evan hadn't moved. He gestured for him to hurry up. Evan chuckled and shook his head before following.

Upon entering the bar, Moses surveyed the space; there was a DJ booth set up and a sound system in the corner. It was almost packed with guests.

'Feel like I still need to warm up,' Julian said. 'It's like we were the first to come but the last to arrive.'

'What time is it?' Moses asked.

Julian checked his watch. 'Nine-thirty.'

'Forget this.' Evan loosened his bow tie. He slinked over to a bartender and asked for a drink of water. When he came back, he took out a packet containing a few pills.

'Come on,' said Julian. 'Already?'

Evan threw a pill into his mouth and drank the water. 'Anyone else?'

'I'm good without it,' Julian replied.

Moses declined with a shake of his head before leading them through the bar and out towards the ballroom, which was the largest room in the house and was where most of the guests were.

On their way, the three of them had passing interactions

with other groups, some of whom were already drunk. Moses noticed they couldn't help coming off as secretive now that they were searching for something they wanted no one else to find. He tried to discern if the people they spoke to were also looking for the secret Benjamin had, but he didn't want to give his intentions away, and he thought that even if others were, they would also be cagey.

For a while, the trio allowed themselves to spend time back in the foyer to enjoy the distractions of the people around them and to pick out interesting parts of the mansion's grand architecture, such as the slick, circular lights hanging from the towering ceiling, which were small but bright. Eventually, Evan suggested they go outside to see if they could find anything special there. They headed to the garden, where it was filling with guests.

'How does Benjamin know this many people?' Evan asked.

'He doesn't,' Moses answered. 'Put a mansion and a party together; what do you think's going to happen?'

'Party?' Julian observed. 'It's a soirée.'

Moses laughed.

'We're stalling,' Julian said, changing the subject. 'I don't know Benjamin as well as you, Moses, which means I might never be in a house like this again, so I want to check out the rest of it, find whatever it is we need to find, then tell him I want his car for doing it.'

Evan tittered. 'That's ambitious. You might need a pill for all of that.'

Julian burst out laughing. Moses, who now wasn't paying much attention to them, saw three women in a corner of the grounds on their phones. One of them, who was in a black outfit and had her hair in locks, caught his eye. She was standing in the middle.

Before Julian and Evan realised what he was doing, he approached them. The middle one glanced up at him then quickly looked away, while the woman beside her, who had a short coat on over her outfit, slowly inspected him as he neared them. She smiled at him, and when he was about to speak she cut him off: 'Hi.' She put her phone away. 'How did you hear about the soirée?'

Moses heard Evan say behind him, 'Told you,' before chuckling. He returned his attention to the woman in front of him, who was now scanning his friends.

'You guys don't sound like you're from here.' Her focus darted towards Julian and Evan again, who had now come closer.

'We're not,' Moses said. 'We're from Wrentpole.'

The woman nodded slowly. 'We're from Cahringham.'

He nodded back. 'Have you guys been to the mansion before?'

The third woman leaned forward. Her hair was brown, and she was in a blue jumpsuit. 'No, but I know Benjamin's sister.'

'What's your name?' the one in the coat asked Moses.

Moses told her. He then pointed to his friends. 'That's Julian, and that's Evan. What's yours?'

'Kelly,' the one in the coat said. Kelly gestured at her friend with locks. 'She's Merissa,' and then she pointed at the third woman in the blue, 'and that's Tara.'

Moses glanced at Merissa. She gave him a faint smile. His eyes picked out a small necklace she had on, but besides that she was wearing no jewellery, unlike the other female guests, who were covered in it. He smiled back.

Julian stepped forward. 'How come you guys aren't inside?'

Kelly shrugged. 'We're just waiting for something to happen.'

Julian glimpsed at his two friends, who glanced back at him. He whispered to the women, 'You guys seem pretty chilled ... Be honest, are you looking for what Benjamin's hidden too?'

Kelly's eyes flicked between Tara and Merissa, and a small grin escaped her.

The six of them continued to talk, about the mansion and what Benjamin might have hidden. The grounds began to fill more, and the route back to the entrance started to get crowded. Julian checked his watch. 'It's ten-fifteen,' he whispered to Moses. 'We won't manage to search the rest of the mansion in time if we stay here. For all we know others might be looking.'

Moses nodded. He turned to the three women, who were still chuckling at something he had said a second ago. 'We're going inside. Julian wants to ...' He trailed off; Julian was already walking back to the mansion.

'Okay,' said Kelly.

'Are you guys staying here?' Moses asked.

Kelly turned to her friends, and they started speaking quietly amongst one another.

After a couple of moments, Evan said, 'We'll see you inside.' He made his way over to Julian, who was now waiting to see if Moses was coming.

Moses returned his attention to Kelly and her friends. 'Catch you later.'

He caught up with Julian and Evan and together they neared the entrance. He studied the garden and the house; the size of it in the night charmed him, and he understood why Julian was eager to see more – regardless of finding what Benjamin had hidden.

His friends were moving quickly to escape the cold air, which they had been able to ignore before due to being immersed in conversation. They entered the foyer once more, and as Moses followed, he felt someone bump into him from behind. He turned around; it was Kelly, followed by Tara and Merissa.

'Yeah,' she said, 'we're coming with you.'

Moses, Julian and Evan approached the grand staircase, accompanied by Kelly, Tara and Merissa, and began to make their way up. As the group reached the second flight of stairs, they heard collective gasping and cheering before realising someone was jumping from the second floor into a pack of people in the foyer below. After exchanging shocked and impressed reactions, they continued upstairs. They reached the top of the east staircase that ended on the second floor then entered the adjacent corridor, where they passed a room that looked like it was reserved for people who had found someone to make out with and wanted to do so without interruption. Moses led the way as they continued further, seeing only a few people, as they descended a flight of stairs before then realising they were now on the far east side of the first floor.

Moses' first inclination was to tell everyone to head back to the ballroom, but Merissa spoke, and at the sound of a voice that had scarcely been heard so far, everyone listened: 'I don't think what he wants us to find is near the ballroom. That's too obvious a place to search. If anything, we probably need to go further away from the party.'

'You're right,' said Moses.

'Why are we looking again?' asked Evan. 'Is he really going to let whoever finds it have whatever they want?'

'That pill's making you impatient,' Julian commented. He glanced at his watch. 'We've got an hour and a bit left anyway. Afterwards, we can let loose.'

Evan rolled his eyes. Tara moved beside him. 'I was thinking the same,' she said to him, 'but you never know; it really might be something special. Besides, everyone's too pissed and busy jumping off stairs to look, so someone has to.'

He grunted.

Moses gestured for them to all continue.

There was nothing much where they were on the first floor, and the only company they had was each other and the sleek décor of the mansion. Moses tried a few doors, which were all locked, and spirits were only raised when Evan finally found one that wasn't. When Evan pushed it open, they all peered inside and saw a room full of bookshelves and framed comics. There was a collective sigh.

Evan lifted a graphic novel. '*Visionary: Volume One,*' he said. 'Neat. You think this could be it?'

Moses shook his head. 'I know him. It'd be more wow than that.'

Evan shoved the comic back where he took it from and closed the door behind him.

Moses led them further on until they reached the end of the west side of the first floor, which ended at a set of stairs connecting to the ground floor. At the bottom, there were guests in dinner suits and sharp dresses moving backwards and forwards. Some were ambling up the stairs where they were, stopping to enjoy moments of laughter, while others were going elsewhere.

Kelly paused. 'Wait, have we been to the west side of the second floor yet?'

Moses shook his head.

'Should we take a look?'

Moses nodded, and the group headed to where she had suggested.

There, it was mostly empty, but it came to life with their conversations as they explored and examined details of the mansion that could be easily missed, like the craftsmanship on the stair rails and the raised patterns on the doors. After passing a few entrances, trying them one by one, they noticed another group of voices. Upon following the winding corridor they saw who the chattering belonged to. It was a mixed group of revellers, like them, who appeared to be slightly drunk by the way they were shouting as one of them tried a door.

Moses slowed, and the others did the same. He watched the other gang quieten as they realised they weren't alone. Silence filled the space between them.

'Hey,' Moses shouted. 'You searching as well?'

A few of them nodded, and one of them, the tallest of the group, spoke, 'Yeah.' He grinned. 'What you going to take if you find it?'

Before Moses could talk, Julian shouted, 'His car.'

The opposing crew cackled, and amongst the loud laughter one of them shouted back, 'I want his fridge.'

Moses found himself chuckling along with the others. Once the shared hilarity passed, he said, 'Good luck,' to the crew opposite.

Evan leaned into Moses' ear. 'Why are we wishing them good luck? They're our competition.' He faced the group, and Moses, knowing what was coming, put his face in his palm. 'I hope you don't find shit,' Evan said.

'Wow.' One of the girls stepped forward. 'Relax. It's just fun.'

'For you maybe,' said Evan, 'but we didn't come all the way from Wrentpole for the thrills. Where here for the spoils too.'

'Oh.' The girl stared at him, blinking, before shaking her head. 'You're from that shitbox. No wonder you're scavenging.'

'What? Shut the—'

'Hey.' Moses put his arm in front of Evan, ready to hold him back. He whispered, 'Chill.'

'Are you hearing them?'

Moses ignored him. 'Wrentpole ain't a shitbox,' he said, 'but there's no need to kick off over this. Like you said, it's just a bit of fun.'

Moses watched the tallest one screw his face up as he was about to respond, but all of the friends around him had begun walking away, and Moses could hear them muttering. He caught the sound of curses under their breaths and thought that whatever rude comments they were making were distasteful descriptions of him and his companions, but he said nothing so as to not encourage Evan and left them to disappear down the hallway.

'I don't care what Benjamin's hidden,' Evan murmured as he marched forward, 'but we're finding it before that lanky prick does.'

Tara giggled, and Moses shook his head at Evan's lack of restraint but had to hold back his own laughter.

As they tried a few more doors, Moses observed his friends and saw Evan was now checking the time in addition to Julian. There was less talking, and he gathered that the encounter with the other group had made what was meant to be a fun quest a competitive search. Now, instead of only one of them trying a door, others would attempt to force it open if one person had failed. After they had almost gone full circle around the second floor, Moses felt himself beginning to grow frustrated. 'I wonder if this is just a joke Benjamin's playing,' he said to no one in particular, 'and we're just the idiots thick enough to take part.'

'It was your idea,' said Julian. 'No turning back now.'

Moses slowed to a stop. 'This is getting exhausting. So what if those other guys find it?' He checked his phone. 'We've got thirty minutes. Come, let's head back. We've missed enough already.'

'Wait.' Merissa's voice made Moses and the others focus in her direction. She was attempting the same door the group they had encountered earlier had tried. She used her weight to push the handle down then pressed her shoulder with force against the door. It creaked open.

Everyone froze.

'Is this his bedroom?' Merissa whispered. They all gathered around her, and the sheer volume of all of them behind her trying to peer in meant she was involuntarily pushed inside. She swore and quickly searched around for the light switch. She found it and pressed it. The lights came on, and they all entered.

Benjamin's room was vast, and there was enough space for all of them to walk around without coming near each other.

'Where's his bed?' asked Tara.

Merissa, who had gone further ahead than the others, pointed. 'There.'

Benjamin's bed was at the end of his room in a large recess, and there was a tall window beside it that presented a clear view of the night outside.

'Imagine having to walk that far into your room just to go to sleep?' Tara added.

'It's a waste of space,' Julian said while he searched for things to go through.

Moses scanned the room. Nothing really stood out, except for a sculpture on his desk of a mother holding a child in what looked like a storm, a tribal mask on the wall and a nearby framed picture of Benjamin with his sister and his parents.

They searched; Evan was being thorough and placing his ear against the wall, much to Tara's amusement, and after five minutes or so, Kelly and Merissa, becoming bored, began heading towards the door, but they stopped when Julian said, 'Found it.'

Julian was at the other end of the room by Benjamin's bed. He was gawking upwards. The others couldn't see what he could because the ceiling of that area was higher than the rest of the bedroom. They hastened towards him and began to utter expressions of astonishment after they had followed his gaze. Moses, who was leaning against Benjamin's desk to rest his legs, swore and pushed himself up when he saw Evan, Tara and Merissa standing on Benjamin's bed to get a better look. He hurried over and shouted at them to come down, but when he caught sight of the painting, he fell silent and studied what he saw above him. 'Wow.' He adjusted his glasses and searched the others' faces. 'Anyone know what that is?'

'I'm seeing fireworks,' Evan answered. 'Wild explosions.'

Tara shook her head. 'You need glasses. It's trees in the autumn. Lots of them fused together.'

'I'm not sure what I see,' said Kelly. 'Every time I blink, I see something different, but I think it's people.'

'I'm thinking the same,' Julian added. 'It's weird, but I'm seeing faces – our faces. It's incredible. Never seen anything like it ... Why wouldn't he tell everyone about this? Everyone in the mansion should see it.'

'Maybe,' Merissa said quietly, 'he thought whoever found it would be his most dedicated friends.'

'Doubt it.' Tara jumped off the bed. 'It could just as well

mean they're the greediest, seeing as you get something for it.'

Merissa climbed down and glanced back up at the painting. 'I don't think so.' She took a picture of it with her phone. 'Only people close to you would have the balls to ransack every room in your house.'

Tara laughed.

'It's true,' Merissa added. 'Regular people might think they were interfering too much if they checked as many places we did.'

'Either way,' Evan said, jumping down, 'we found it. This is definitely it.'

Moses stared upwards. 'It is. I'll ask him about it.' He checked the time. 'Fifteen minutes left.' He glanced at everyone. 'Who wants something from the mansion then?'

Evan turned to Julian. 'Are you still going to ask for his car?'

Julian gave him an unamused look. 'I was joking.'

'I'm going to look round and see if I find anything that grabs me,' said Tara. She wandered away from the bed and started going through Benjamin's things.

Moses ground his teeth as he watched the others do the same. He sent a text message to Benjamin telling him that he thought he'd found whatever it was he wanted the guests to discover. He leaned against Benjamin's bed as he waited for a reply and kept an eye on his friends as they investigated the room. He caught Merissa opening a drawer of Benjamin's desk and taking out some documents.

'Hey,' he said as he walked over, 'let's not take the piss.'

Merissa ignored him and shuffled through the papers. 'He's been to the hospital a lot.' She dropped the papers back in the drawer before turning around and closing it with her hip and then resting against it. She stared at Moses.

'You enjoying yourself?' he asked.

'I am. You?'

'I would be … If I didn't have to police you guys.'

Merissa smirked.

Before Moses could say more, Kelly approached them. 'Your mate Benjamin is a weird one. All that money, and all he's got is a two-page spread from a comic on his ceiling.'

Kelly smiled and tried to stop herself laughing. It was infectious, and Moses found himself holding back laughter.

'You're cruel,' he said. 'It's obviously a painting.'

They both chuckled. Moses noticed Merissa leave as Kelly began to talk about the image, and while she spoke, Julian crept up to them, wearing the mask that had been on the wall. He said something the two of them couldn't hear because of his face being covered.

He took it off. 'There's not much here. I wouldn't expect to see a painting like that in a room this minimalistic … I wonder how whoever did it got up there.'

'With a ladder?' Kelly suggested. 'But I'm just guessing.'

Julian stared at her. 'Is that sarcasm?'

She smiled.

Evan appeared and picked up the sculpture of the mother and child, which was behind Moses. 'I think this is what I'm taking.' He clumsily swung around to show it to everyone and bumped into Tara, who had come up behind him, which caused him to lose his grip of it. Moses was already in front of him and caught it before it dropped.

'C'mon,' Moses said. He placed the sculpture on the table as far away from Evan as possible. 'Let's leave.'

He headed towards the doorway and gestured for the others to follow.

They were all still talking about the painting as they proceeded further along the corridor. Moses, who was ahead of the others, was quiet, and through the voices of his friends he thought he could hear two people speaking in another room not far from them. He walked ahead.

'Why are you rushing?' Evan shouted.

Moses approached the open door of what was a large bathroom and could hear the voices of Benjamin and his sister, Krista. He edged towards the entrance then peered around the door and discovered Benjamin sitting on some steps with a towel in one hand and a glass of water in the other. Krista was sat behind him, with one arm draped over the centre of his chest while her free hand gently stroked his hair. The sound of a running tap filled the room. Krista produced a pill and brought it to Benjamin's lips. He swallowed it then raised the glass to his mouth.

'Are you okay?' she said.

Benjamin's voice was hoarse. 'Yeah.'

Krista hugged him, and he held her hands. She leaned down and kissed him on the cheek. He shifted his head slightly, as if he knew they were being watched, and Moses froze when his eyes fell on him.

'Hey,' Benjamin said. He dabbed his mouth with the towel. 'Sorry for being absent hosts. I've been exhausted.'

Krista smiled, but Moses thought he could see that she was concealing sadness.

'Have you been enjoying it?' she asked.

'Yeah, we have.' Moses felt Julian and Evan behind him, and he was shunted further into the bathroom.

Benjamin nodded. 'You guys found it.' He winked at them.

'It's nice,' said Evan. He gestured to the ceiling as if they were still in the bedroom. 'What's the painting?'

Benjamin grinned. 'It's everything and everyone.' He stood up slowly. His bow tie was undone, and he positioned himself in front of a mirror and tied it. 'You can tell me what you want on the way downstairs – I'm going to show my face for a bit, then I'm going to make a speech.'

He headed out of the bathroom. Krista locked the tap and then followed. Kelly, Tara and Merissa made way for the pair as they came out, before trailing behind the two of them, both tall and statuesque, as they continued down the corridor.

'So,' Kelly whispered to Moses as he joined them, 'what was that all about?'

Moses shook his head. 'Don't know.'

'Told you,' she said. 'They're weird.'

There was a gap between Benjamin and Krista and the group behind them as they made their way down the grand staircase and into the ballroom, which had grown even livelier. Once they were inside, Benjamin asked Kelly, Tara and Merissa if there was anything they wanted for discovering the painting. Tara shook her head and Merissa did too.

'We're fine.' Kelly answered. 'It was just a bit of fun. We've spent enough time searching the mansion. It's about time the party started for us.'

'Okay,' Benjamin said.

Kelly wrapped her arms around Tara and Merissa and steered them towards the bar.

'You're paying for the first round,' said Merissa, causing Kelly's eyes to widen. 'You're the one who decided we should spend all that time following them around.'

'I agree,' Tara added.

Kelly grunted. She let go of them and marched to the bar with Tara and Merissa laughing behind her.

'What now?' Moses asked Benjamin.

'Going to catch a few people then go to the rooftop so I can talk to everyone. Want to come? It's going to be cold up there.'

Krista made a noise imitating a shiver before wrapping her arms around herself. 'Cold? I'll give that a miss.' She placed a hand on her brother's arm. 'I'm going to find some friends who I haven't had a chance to see yet.' She pointed at the others. 'I'll see the rest of you from the garden.'

As soon as Krista left, Moses saw guests who she knew approach her, and she disappeared with them.

Moses tugged the lapels of his jacket. 'I'll come.'

Benjamin turned to Julian and Evan.

They exchanged glances. 'Why not?' Julian said. 'It'll be a good view.'

'Yeah,' said Benjamin, 'it will.'

On their way to the roof, Benjamin was held up repeatedly by eager guests who wanted to congratulate him on the party and have a conversation with him. Moses, Julian and Evan soon realised just how many people were in the house, and just how many of them Benjamin knew personally. They glanced at each other as people constantly pulled him to one side, and it took him so long to remove himself each time that they doubted Benjamin would ever get to the rooftop. Eventually, once all who wanted Benjamin had had a chance to speak with him, they were free to make their way down the west corridor of the second floor. By then, several people had offered Benjamin drinks, seeing as he was without one, but he declined. Benjamin pulled a microphone from his inside jacket pocket as he took the trio through one of the rooms on the second floor, ignoring the loitering guests who were present. He used a key to unlock a door that led onto a balcony. From there, there was a narrow staircase leading to the roof, and they all proceeded to climb up it, one behind the other.

As they did so, Moses said to Benjamin, 'Your room.'

'I'll tell you all about that later. And don't worry, you'll be able to take whatever you want, as promised.'

They reached the roof. It was mostly flat, and they could hardly see in the immediate darkness, save for the triangular shapes of the solar panels that took up much of the space.

'What are we doing?' Julian whispered to Moses.

Moses didn't have an answer. He could hear the others' breathing, with the exception of Benjamin, who was now walking further ahead towards the lights that were glowing at the back of the mansion. The voices of the guests outside the house reminded him of the sound of the ocean. Ahead, the outline of the trees was veiled in mist, and in the darkness the shapes were two-dimensional, akin to a cardboard cut-out below the screen of the night.

They carried on until they were at the rear of the roof over-looking the garden. Benjamin walked to the very edge, while the others stood close enough that they could see the people below illuminated by the exterior lights but not so close that one step meant they would fall.

Moses found it difficult to recognise any of the faces from the height they were at, and he wasn't sure if anyone below would recognise them either.

Benjamin pushed a button on his microphone then typed a message on his mobile. 'To the dude in charge of the sound,' he explained. His phone lit up as he received a reply. The music from the speakers outside turned off, and he smiled.

He lifted the microphone and hesitated for a moment before saying, 'Hey.'

Benjamin's voice came out of the speakers within the house as well as those outside the mansion before rippling through the air and disappearing into the distance. Immediately, Moses heard the elated voices from the guests increase in volume and then quieten as they focused on where the omnipresent sound had come from. He watched Benjamin gaze down, not at the people, but at the area directly beneath him.

'I'm your host,' he eventually said, 'Benjamin Kind.'

Moses knew that his friend's act of putting on a party in such a magnificent setting would warrant some cheers, and he couldn't help grinning as people started to do just that.

Benjamin continued. 'I'm glad you're here ... all of you.'

The vibrations of his voice gently shook Moses' insides, and he noticed Benjamin was shaking slightly as his utterances were projected. A cold wind swept past, stinging Moses when it touched his skin.

'I've been planning this for some time,' Benjamin added. 'After the way things have been for so many years now, and how it's finally getting better, something like this is a relief; celebrating being able to celebrate, and to see so many people here from so many places, and to share it with all of you, means a lot.' Benjamin stared into the microphone. 'I want everyone to realise that they're a part of something, a part of something beyond themselves.'

'What's he talking about?' Evan whispered to Moses.

'And it's this.' Benjamin put his hand out and moved it horizontally as if he was levelling something with his palm. 'This here is a pool, a pool of collective history, experience and emotion.' He brought his hand to his heart. There was silence. He pointed down with his finger. 'I want you to internalise this night, the feelings, the people you've met, but most importantly I want you to preserve this occasion and those who made it possible, so that it's a part of you, kept somewhere deeper than your memory ... and to keep me, your host, Benjamin, there beside it.'

Silence.

Benjamin breathed in, and Moses thought he was going to speak again at length.

'Lastly ... congratulations to Moses, Julian and Evan, and Kelly, Tara and Merissa, for finding the special something that was hidden in the mansion. They're true friends ... Thank you, everyone.' He turned the microphone off, and the crowd applauded.

Moses and the others watched him amble to the steps that led back into the mansion.

They followed and could still hear the excited response from the guests below.

'That was kind of philosophical,' Julian said as they re-entered the house. 'I didn't understand it all, but still.'

Benjamin was quiet.

'What were you saying out there?' Moses asked.

'And your room,' Evan said. 'That mural.'

Benjamin said nothing until they reached the second-floor west staircase, where he stopped and sat on the top step. The others settled beside him or a few steps below. They could hear that most of the guests were now on the ground floor, having rushed out to hear what was happening when Benjamin made his speech. Benjamin was staring down at his feet, and the three of them observed him, waiting for him to speak.

'Before anything,' he said, 'let me know what each of you want.'

'*Visionary: Volume One*,' Evan said.

Benjamin made a short chuckle.

'I know my history,' Evan added. 'That'll be worth something in a few years.'

'It's yours.'

'This is why everyone loves you, man ... Julian said he wants your—'

'Shut up,' said Julian, and Evan doubled over with laughter. 'I want that tribal mask, or that sculpture ... The one Evan almost broke.'

Evan glared at Julian.

'Have both,' Benjamin said.

Julian's eyes widened. 'Are you sure?'

'I've had it for years. I barely look at it now, but it's a good reminder of what people went through during those times.'

Moses spoke before Benjamin had a chance to ask. 'I don't want anything.'

'Except for Merissa,' said Evan. 'We've seen you trying to catch a moment with her.'

Moses tried to conceal a smile. 'The night's not over yet … We might all get what we want in the end.'

Evan laughed.

Benjamin was the first to fall silent. 'That mural,' he said after a while, 'represents all of us, the unconscious space we all share.'

The three of them glanced at each other, and Moses knew they were all eager for Benjamin to clarify.

Benjamin clenched his fists. 'I wanted to say more, about how life and experience can live inside that space, so even if you've never met me – or even when I'm gone – you can learn from my history because you already share my spirit.' Benjamin touched Moses' arm and stared at all of them. 'You're not aware of it, but you do. You all do.'

Benjamin let go of Moses. He rested his elbows on his thighs and watched between his feet. He shook his head and breathed out. 'I'm ill.'

Moses, Julian and Evan looked at one another. Evan leaned forward, and Moses thought he was about to interrupt so fired a warning look his way that told him to keep quiet so Benjamin could finish.

Benjamin brought his hand to his forehead. 'I just want to keep the connections I have. The ceiling painting I had done so I could see everyone I know when I wake up, while I still have time, see them all together.' He studied his friends. 'The rooftop, really, that was a farewell. I wanted to say something that would resonate without it being a sob story or sounding selfish.' He sat up slightly. 'I forgot some of it. You probably didn't notice, but it didn't have the punch I wanted.' He rubbed his face then pushed himself up and gave them a smile that was warmer than both his tone and what he was saying. 'Don't let my morbid state ruin your night.'

Moses and the others were quiet.

'That's the last thing I want today to be. I just wanted everyone together, and I did that … Still, I would've liked something more to happen.'

'Like what?' Moses said.

Benjamin started down the steps and was holding onto the rail. 'Good question … I don't know. Maybe I shouldn't ask for more. Everyone being here is enough.'

'Will you get better?' Julian asked.

Benjamin paused. 'I'm not sure … Everyone else seems to have hope, but … I don't know.'

He made his way down the stairs. 'And get yourselves downstairs,' he added. 'It's about time you enjoyed the soirée.'

Moses, Julian and Evan started towards the ballroom in search for the enjoyment that Benjamin had instructed them to find. They wandered around the intoxicated people on the grand staircase who had ended up slumped there with their heads between their knees, and in the entrance hall they saw Krista perched on a cabinet that was too big for her to have climbed onto herself. She was singing to a group of onlookers below who were cheering her on.

Moses watched her as she sang, thinking about her brother, until she noticed him and waved.

They entered the ballroom and went around the revellers to the back. Despite the collective loss of inhibition, there was still a certain level of control amongst the guests, which Moses thought was due to the respect that the mansion commanded.

Evan took the packet of pills out of his pocket again. 'My buzz is wearing. I need water.'

The three of them left the ballroom to find drinks. They saw a large crew of finely dressed guests coming down the corridor led by Benjamin, who was now laughing and taking sips from a glass of wine. When Benjamin reached them, he slowed down and inspected them. Evan continued into the bar.

'Moses,' Benjamin said, 'I told you to loosen up.' He took a bottle from the person next to him and shoved it in Moses' hand.

'We are. We're still warming up.' Moses felt the bottle being pulled; Julian was taking it from him.

'Better than waiting in line,' Julian said as he put it to his mouth.

Benjamin grinned. He entered the bar and the group behind him followed.

Moses wrestled the bottle from Julian and drank from it before passing it back.

Shouting erupted.

They checked the counter at the bar; Evan was being held back by strangers while another group of men and women, who were also being restrained, yelled at him. Moses recognised them instantly as the people they had seen searching for the mural earlier. He ran forward with Julian and shoved them just as they broke free and tried to attack Evan. Julian punched one who swung for him in the face, and Benjamin shouted for them to stop while pushing Moses away.

'You're a prick,' the tallest one of the gang shouted. 'Acting high and mighty 'cause you found a picture. Wait in fucking line like everyone else.'

Evan raised his middle finger at him. Moses and Julian were being forced back as they swore and shouted.

The altercation soon took on a life of its own, and the opposing side were still angry and wanted a chance to pay Moses and Julian back for jumping into the conflict, but the trio were now surrounded by a growing crowd of guests who were supporting them.

Moses didn't recognise any of them but gathered they felt the need to get involved because they were who Benjamin had congratulated for finding what was hidden in the mansion.

When things finally started to cool, Moses suggested to Julian and Evan that they all go outside.

'No,' Evan said. 'I'm staying here. I'm not looking like a pussy.'

Moses swore under his breath.

Julian neared him and whispered, 'I'm staying too. It's not

a good idea to leave him on his own, but if you want to go outside for a bit you should.'

Moses nodded. 'Alright ... Just keep your shit together.'

He made his way out to the garden, and as he entered he found himself looking out for Merissa. Outside, he tightened his tie and untucked his shirt. He took his glasses off and cleaned them with his jacket sleeve. When he put them back on, he saw that one of his shoelaces was loose, and he walked over to a corner of the garden before crouching down and tying them. He noticed a presence in front of him and glanced up. It was Kelly and Tara.

'Why are you by yourself?' Kelly asked.

Moses finished tying his laces and stood up. 'I'm not. Just came out for some air.'

'If you say so.'

'What you doing now?'

'We don't know,' Kelly said. 'We're kind of scattered ... and a bit drunk.'

She came closer and reached for Moses' arm. She started pulling him back to the mansion while walking backwards, and Moses saw Tara's expression turn into one of annoyance as she watched. A gust of wind blew Kelly's hair into her face. It seemed almost white against the darkness as it caught the light from the mansion. Moses stared at her; she was smiling as she tried to smooth her hair back. Her teeth were clear to the point that they were almost radiant, and without the constant distraction of the others, Moses had a moment to consider things he hadn't thought about before – involuntarily picking out features of hers he hadn't acknowledged but that now held his attention, such as her earrings, which resembled gold droplets of water. It reminded him of the way he had noticed Merissa's necklace. Having Kelly's friend in his mind again made him ask, 'Where's Merissa?'

Kelly shrugged. 'I think she tried to find a way to the rooftop after hearing Benjamin give that public service announcement.'

Moses chuckled.

'She never wanted to come, you know?' She was slurring slightly. 'I think she's tired of us dragging her around.' She and Tara both laughed.

'One moment. I'm just going to check up on Evan and Julian.' He headed back into the mansion, without giving the two women a chance to stop him.

He popped into the bar to quickly see how Julian and Evan were; Julian was nursing his knuckles, and Evan was sitting near him with his head between his thighs while holding a bottle. Seeing that they were somewhat coping, Moses made his way to the grand staircase. He followed the route Benjamin had taken when he'd led them to the roof to see if maybe he would find Merissa on the way.

Moses glimpsed across the mansion rooftop but could make out no one in the near darkness. He was met with the distant view of Benjamin's park-sized garden. He peered around as he ventured further onto the roof in the hope that Kelly hadn't lied about Merissa.

He put his hands in his pockets, and as he neared the edge, he saw the shape of someone sitting down. The way their hair was arranged made him realise it was Merissa. Moses stepped forward, but she didn't notice him as he approached. When he was beside her, he spoke. 'Can you see my friends from here?'

Merissa jolted. She pressed a hand against her chest and breathed out. 'You scared me. No, I can't.'

'Same. We're too high up.'

Merissa turned her attention to the view. 'Were you on the rooftop earlier?'

Moses grinned. 'You noticed me from there?'

Smiling, she bit her bottom lip and looked away from him. 'I noticed all of you.'

Moses sat down. 'You came up here by yourself?'

'Do you see anyone else here?'

He shook his head and focused on the crowd below in the garden.

'You're afraid of heights?' she said.

'Who isn't?'

'I'm not; the view makes it worth it.'

Moses returned to the scene in the garden. The movement of the spots that were the guests created a picture animated with detail.

'Why are you alone?' Merissa asked.

'Everyone else is burned out ... Why are you? I saw Kelly and Tara a few moments ago.'

Merissa didn't reply. He thought he saw her roll her eyes. A cold breeze touched them, and he watched her hands clench and her body tense until it passed.

'This is really quite high,' he commented.

She glanced at him.

'When we were with Benjamin, we were at a distance.

Well, I was.' He looked down and quickly leaned back. 'But this is a lot closer.'

Merissa peered down. 'It is.'

'Why are you on the very edge anyway?'

'How often am I on a mansion rooftop? Got to make the most of it.'

'True. Still, being this high up isn't something I'm—'

'Why are you talking to me?'

Moses froze. 'What?'

'You barely said a word to me before, so why are you sitting with me now, on a rooftop, while there's a party below us and you could be down there with Kelly or Tara?'

'You didn't talk much, so—'

'Just answer the question,' she said quietly.

Moses thought he wasn't meant to hear it, but before he could speak, she continued.

'Kelly likes you … I think she wants to fuck you by the end of the night.'

'Really?' Moses chuckled. 'Okay … She said you didn't want to be here. How come?'

'Why'd you think? Not my kind of thing, a wild soirée,' she used her fingers to imitate quotation marks, 'loads of drugs and surrounded by people who are damn near royalty.'

Moses laughed loudly, which caused Merissa to grin.

'Are you going back down to the ballroom?'

She shrugged. 'Don't know. I'm only here 'cause those two forced me to come. I've been looking for a place to escape to all night. That's kind of why I agreed with Kelly to follow you in the search … to get away from it all.' She glanced around. 'Anyway, Kelly isn't here, so you'd better go back.'

For a moment, Moses was silent. 'But you are.'

Merissa was watching her feet slowly swing. 'So?'

After Moses didn't respond, Merissa turned to look him in the eye. 'And?'

'And you're not very sociable, are you? I thought if I got your friends to like me then you would too, but from the looks of it that didn't work, did it?'

Her eyes widened. She covered her mouth and started to laugh.

Moses gazed down into the garden for a moment. He could feel her watching him.

'Are you still scared?'

'Of the height? I never was. Who told you otherwise?' He faked leaning over the edge before quickly bringing himself back up, and Merissa giggled.

'What was your friend talking about earlier?'

'He was talking about … how we're all part of the same unconscious space.'

'Oh. I wasn't listening.'

'He was saying it's why we share the same experiences and history. More now than ever since the storm, I guess.'

There was a silence between them. A mist was shrouding the moon, but the light from Benjamin's mansion was enough for them to see below.

'That sounds interesting, but I doubt someone like Benjamin has shared the experiences we've had – storm or no storm. Definitely not the same history, shared unconsciousness or not … He really is a weird guy.'

Moses stared at her. He thought about what Benjamin had said on the stairs about being ill, and he felt himself becoming irritated by Merissa's words. 'He isn't weird. He just wants to live.'

'What?'

He pushed himself up. He couldn't hide his shuddering as he leered at the distant garden below. 'Watch how everyone reacts.' He started waving his hands. After a couple of seconds, he saw those in the garden start to look up.

Merissa chuckled. 'Stop it.'

He continued waving his arms.

'What are you doing?'

'Proving Benjamin's right.'

The music stopped abruptly, and he could hear voices rising.

'Don't.'

He ignored her.

'You're going to scare people.'

Before he could reply, his attention was caught by someone screaming, 'Go on! Do it!'

'More like the opposite,' he then said as Merissa leaned over with a shocked expression as she tried to find who had shouted.

'We want you to jump,' someone yelled.

'You're not going to kill yourself,' Merissa said.

'No, but I would've proved Benjamin was right.' Moses stepped backwards as if he was trying to create enough distance so that he could run and leap off.

'How? You know what? You're right; he's right. You can sit down now.'

'Do it,' someone below shouted, and a chant repeating those same two words began.

Merissa got to her feet and darted towards Moses. She grabbed his arm. 'Let's go inside.'

The chants turned into boos, and Moses smirked.

'Stop smiling.'

'You want me to do it. I can hear it in your voice.'

Merissa hesitated.

'You do.' He fixed his attention to the light coming from the house, which was below the night and closer to the sound of people on the ground. 'Everyone does; you want an opportunity to a tell a story about how someone jumped off a mansion rooftop.'

Merissa shook her head, and he saw the moisture on her mouth glisten as she bit her bottom lip.

'You're trying not to smile.'

Merissa laughed loudly. 'You're being ridiculous. Please, come back.'

Below them, the guests were still chanting. The garden was even fuller now; it seemed everyone had poured out of the house to see what was happening.

Merissa continued to pull at his arm. 'Really, don't. You're assuming they'll catch you.'

Moses moved further back. 'Doesn't matter. If I jump, then whenever they think about the rash or the overconfident they'll think of me – you'll all think of me. I'll be more than a memory. I'll represent something – recklessness. That's what Benjamin was trying to say, how he wants to represent something.'

Moses stepped back again so that he was further from Merissa and far enough from the edge that he could build momentum if he were to run. He crouched slightly, assuming a running stance, and Merissa let go of him, allowing him to. He gazed out at Benjamin's grounds and at the darkness that possessed an edge of brightness due to the mansion's exterior lights. The chant was still continuing, and the voice of the guests intertwined with the air, becoming a vibration that sounded natural, something Moses knew he was familiar with, despite never having heard anything like it.

Soulmate

We said the conflict started due to faith, because of natural disaster and over food, but in our subconscious we knew it was something more. It was about affection, never having the opportunity to create an environment where we could experience it; never having the means to obtain it.

In our first fight, we learned about fear and the pain of loss. The fighting became about retribution, rather than the war we had begun so that we could find a soulmate and start a life with them. Without losing them to the struggle for basic needs.

We took up arms. We killed. We became monsters.

When peace finally washed away the blood, we let our weapons go, and we looked at those who we had wanted to be reflections of our compassion and saw in the mirror of their eyes that we were now ugly; they broken by our war, and us no longer worthy of the affection we had fought to win.

A Stroke of Madness

HIL PARK

Amri reached forward with his shears and cut off a branch. A few metres away, Carl was doing the same. Traffic whipped past behind them, and whenever it was a bus or truck approaching, a rush of air would arise along with small bits of dirt that would sometimes bounce off Amri's workwear.

Carl spoke loudly across the distance, 'I went shopping with the kids on the weekend. Everywhere you look there's construction.'

Amri nodded so that Carl knew he was listening.

'People complain about the redevelopment,' he added, 'but they're knocking down abandoned buildings, renovating old ones and planting more trees, so what's the problem?' When Amri didn't answer, Carl glanced at him. He spoke slowly, 'And have you seen what they're doing with Hil Park?'

'I think I've heard, but I haven't seen.'

'They're building a block of flats there – fancy ones. Not sure how much of the park'll be left, but they'll probably leave some of it to give it that modern finish. Fuck anyone complaining, I say. That place was a hovel for smackheads and litter. The second they want to do something with it, people start moaning, but these are the same people who never used it in the first place.'

Amri dragged a long branch out of the hedge.

'It was a shithole,' Carl said.

'Yeah.'

'How's Kali?'

'She's good.'

'I keep saying it, but I'm glad you got custody.'

'Yeah.'

'If I ever got divorced like you did, I'd—'

'Carl, leave it.'

Taken aback, Carl raised his hands slightly to show he was retreating from the subject. He moved further down the road and began attending to a different area.

Amri remained in the same spot, cutting the same place again and again, as he thought about what Carl had said regarding Hil Park. He only realised he had cut too much of the hedge when it was too late.

When Amri arrived home, he could hear the sound of Kali's music from outside the house. He opened the front door, and the music volume dropped.

'Hi Dad.'

The music returned to its previous level.

'Have you eaten?' Amri shouted.

The volume dropped again. 'Yeah,' his daughter said, before increasing it once more.

'Why not just keep it down?' Amri whispered to himself as he removed his workwear. He sauntered up the stairs. Kali's door was open, and he stuck his head round it. 'I'm not liking this song.'

Kali changed the track. She was still in her school uniform.

'I didn't know you enjoyed school that much.'

'I don't. I'm practising a new way of doing my tie.'

Amri watched his daughter as she copied the instructions of a stylist in a video on her computer screen. 'I don't like this one either.'

Kali changed the song again, and when it started, Amri gave her a thumbs up and headed to his room.

On Amri's windowsill, there was a picture of him when he was fourteen, standing beside his older sister, Adea, who was sixteen at the time. In the photo, her confident smile was on show, and she was wearing a large puffer jacket that was glistening because of the rain, while Amri had his hands raised slightly to stop the rainfall getting in his face. Amri picked it up and laid it beside his pillow. Opening the browser on his phone, he logged into several of his social profiles. He entered the name Adea into the search boxes, but none of the faces that appeared was his sister's. The few who bore some resemblance he had messaged in the past, asking them if they had ever lived with the Subira family and telling them that he had a sister with the same name who had gone missing twenty years ago in the storm. They had all answered with apologies for not being able to help.

After scrolling through page after page and being unable to find anything different, he pushed his phone aside and returned the picture of him and his sister to the windowsill.

It was bright but cold outside, and Amri walked with his hands in his pockets until he reached Hil Park. Once he was at the sparse rubble and grass that marked the start of the development, he began scrutinising the construction hoarding that shielded the work that was taking place. There was an information board in front of the panels, which he studied. He read about the new blocks of apartments that were being built, before wandering around the park, which was now partly shrouded by the hoarding. He thought back to the brief demonstrations he had heard about several months before. It was only now he realised that the opposition to the creation of the flats had been defeated.

He clenched his fists and listened to the banging of machines and the shouting of workmen occurring behind the panels. The areas of the park that weren't concealed were covered in litter and uneven grass, but much of it was still untouched while the skeleton of a structure was being erected in its midst.

When Amri woke the following morning, he entered the kitchen and took a small knife from one of the drawers before strolling back upstairs and into his bedroom. He faced the part of the wall nearest his doorway. Scratches of paint flicked off the wall as he cut into it. His hand shook slightly as he felt the density of the surface, but he managed to make a small line before pulling the knife out and digging it into the wall again. He heard Kali's footsteps approaching as she came from her room. She was saying something, but her words failed to pierce his focus. Amri began to carve another line.

'Dad?'

He glanced at her.

'What are you doing?'

He faced the wall again and forced the knife into it. There was a rough snick as it split the surface, and the faint smell of paint tickled his nose. When he finished forming the line, he glimpsed to his left. Kali was still there. She had a jumper and shorts on and was wearing pink and white high-top trainers. Amri thought they were big enough to be boots and that she would've looked ridiculous if her jumper and shorts hadn't had bits of pink in them as well. Her hair was tied into two buns, and her fingernails were painted in clear nail varnish and neatly cut.

'Are you alright?'

Kali raised an eyebrow at him. 'Are you?'

Her eyes moved to the wall. She stared at the lines he'd carved, and her mouth fell open. She stuttered, 'Dad, what are you doing?'

He continued to stare at his daughter. She took a step back.

'If Mum knew you were doing this she'd be mad at you. Really mad.'

Amri was quiet, and Kali inched away until she reached the stairs. He heard her stop halfway down.

'Dad, I hope your sister comes back, but it's been a long time ... I think she's gone.'

He listened to Kali run down the rest of the stairs and out of the house. He could still feel her presence, and it gradually affected his concentration, so that when he raised his arm, he struggled to cut another line. Eventually, he lowered his hand and chucked the knife onto his bed.

Amri and Carl were both wearing Holmefield football team scarves and large coats. They were approaching the stadium with Carl's son, Max, who was excitedly talking about the pending game and asking if his dad would buy him some food when they got inside.

'Don't worry,' Carl said, 'I'll get you something.'

Amri chuckled. 'Will you? The food costs more than a ticket.'

Carl shrugged.

'I had a look at Hil Park yesterday,' Amri said.

'Did you?'

'Yeah.'

'I thought I struck a nerve when I mentioned it.'

'Don't worry. I always think about it.'

There was a silence. As they neared the stadium Amri spoke again. 'There's always a chance there could be some evidence there. What they're doing now might destroy it.'

'Have you asked them to look again?'

'The builders?'

'Not the builders, the police.'

'They've looked, years ago, and they found nothing.'

'How long's it been now?'

Amri didn't answer.

'You shouldn't think about it too much – not like you can help it, but there's nothing you can do about it, is there?

People tried protesting, and that didn't work, so unless you're willing to pull it down then—' Carl stopped. 'I don't know. I don't know what to say, to be honest. I'm going to stop talking.'

Max shouted that they were going to miss the kick-off. Amri watched the floor as they neared the turnstiles. His eyes traced the patterns in the concrete, and he wondered if there had been woodland before the stadium, like Hil Park, and if the bodies of missing loved ones had been lost because of it.

'Are you alright?' asked Carl.

Amri rubbed his eyes with his knuckles. 'I'm fine. Just thinking.'

'Okay.' Carl tightened his scarf and rubbed his hands together. 'Boy, this weather's cutting. How come you didn't ask Kali to come?'

Amri glanced at Carl and laughed. 'She doesn't think football's an excuse to look good, so she's not a fan.'

'Seriously?'

Amri nodded.

'Really?' Carl shook his head. 'She needs to learn her history. I can't think of a more dapper crowd.'

The only light bulb in the basement hung crooked. It emitted a weak glow above Amri, who was sitting at a small table, searching through web pages and forums that explained how to create explosives at home.

He heard Kali calling him from behind the slightly open basement door. He minimised the web tabs. 'Come in.'

'Are you sure?'

'Yeah.'

She strolled in. 'What you doing down here?'

'Nothing. You should've come to the match. It was good. People looked sharp.'

'Really?'

'Really.'

'I can't imagine that.'

'You weren't there.'

'Does it matter, Dad? We lost four nil.'

Amri playfully looked to his left and right in search of some kind of response to her, but he found none, and Kali giggled.

'Why are you down here? It's dusty, and I'm sure several generations of spiders live here.'

'You wouldn't be interested.'

'Dad?'

'I'm serious.'

'Mum said before she left that if you started behaving weird, I should tell her.'

Amri gritted his teeth. 'What's wrong with that woman? Even when she's not here she thinks she can still pull the strings.'

'I know, Dad. I haven't told her anything.'

'There's nothing to tell.'

Kali glanced away.

'Please, don't worry about me. Anyway, did you learn that tie?'

'No, not yet. It's too hard.'

'What was it called?'

'The truelove knot.'

Amri tried to hide a chuckle but failed.

'I knew you were going to laugh.' Kali reached for her dad's laptop and turned it round.

He glimpsed at the screen and lifted his hand. He was about to stop her from raising the lowered tab, but when he saw her open a fresh window he pulled his arm back.

'I'll show you it. I've never seen anyone in school with it, none of the girls – or boys even. I think I'll be the first woman to tie one.'

'Trendsetter.'

'Watch all the girls copy me afterwards.' She typed true-love knot in the search bar.

'It's late.' He nodded at the digital clock in the corner of the screen. 'You should be in bed.'

'I know, but when you see it, you'll know why I'm trying to learn it.'

'Because it looks good?'

'Obviously, but like I said, I've never seen anyone else with it – ever.'

Amri leaned forward as Kali showed him the knot. 'Looks pretty cool.'

'I told you,' Kali shouted. 'And you were laughing at me.'

'Tell me when you get the hang of it.'

'I will.'

Amri watched her spin round and skip out of the basement.

A STROKE OF MADNESS

When Amri returned home after work, the house was quiet. He made his way upstairs until he could hear the high-pitched sound of music coming from Kali's headphones. He peeped into her room; she was going through her things and there was a pile of discarded clothes in the corner.

'You having a clear-out?'

She glanced at him but didn't answer. He thought about entering and telling her to remove her headphones but decided not to.

Before he went to sleep that night, Amri rested on his bed with his laptop. He had several tabs open, each with a different social profile he had made, and he entered Adea in the search boxes again and scrolled through the results. He searched until he fell asleep, leaving his laptop screen open on a dating site showing the results of the matches for his sister's name.

Kali appeared in the kitchen doorway as Amri was eating breakfast. She was carrying a rucksack and had her hair tied back in a ponytail, and she wore a black puffer jacket and black trainers along with ripped black jeans. She took a packet of crisps out of the cupboard without looking at her father then made her way out but paused when she reached the doorway.

'What do you think?'

'You're speaking to me now?'

Kali caught herself. 'No, I'm not … You keep counting on your wall, and I'm trying to stop you by not talking to you.'

Amri sat up straighter.

Kali glanced down. 'But at this rate I won't ever be able to speak to you again, which is impossible. And I wouldn't ask you, but there's no one else here.'

Amri spooned some more cereal into his mouth.

'No milk?'

'Not when it's chocolate cereal.'

Kali shook her head as she watched her dad chew. 'Anyway, this is a different look for me. I need to know what people's first impression will be before I leave the house.'

'I can't guess what crowd you fit into this time, honestly.'

'Dad, please.'

He tilted his head. 'You're one of the cool kids?'

'Yeah, but be more specific.'

He scratched his chin. 'You look like a fashion guru who's taken the day off but can't help looking better than the rest.'

Kali's smile turned into a smirk.

She left the kitchen, but a moment later she returned and hovered in the doorway. 'Dad?'

Amri looked up.

'Don't think about your sister too much. I'm sure if she's around she'll be looking for you just as hard as you're looking for her. She might have a tally on her wall too.'

Amri lowered his spoon. He surveyed Kali. 'You remind me of her – Adea.'

Kali froze. 'Do I? Why?'

'She was self-assured as well, always had to have the best piece of clothing – like you, expensive coats and all.' He watched his daughter's eyes light up. 'It's true. She was fashionable, well presented. So, yeah … she was pretty vain too.' He tittered as he chewed on more cereal.

Kali frowned at him but eventually managed a small smile.

'Have a good time at your mum's. I'll pick you up on Sunday evening.'

'Okay.' Kali pivoted round and headed out of the kitchen. 'Try not to stress too much, Dad,' she shouted, and her voice faded as she got further away.

Amri listened to the front door close then sat back and wondered if there was truth in what his daughter had said about his sister.

Carl was staring down at his stomach. 'I don't know how I've got this belly, given all the physical work I do.'

Amri chuckled.

'Seriously, I've put weight on. I think it's my age – slowing metabolism and all.'

'How old are you again?'

'Thirty-seven.'

'Maybe it is age, but you don't look different.'

'You see me most days. My fattening's been gradual, so you haven't noticed. If you put me now next to me from last year, you'd see the difference.'

The two of them reached the truck, and Amri slipped his shovel into the back.

'Honestly, I'm decaying. I can feel it. I'm finding it a bit more difficult to tie my laces without sitting down.'

Amri laughed.

'How you doing?' Carl asked.

Amri stared at Carl, and Carl stared back at him. 'I'm good.'

'Good.' Carl threw his shovel in the back of the truck.

Amri leaned against the tailgate. Carl did the same.

'It's been a long time,' Carl said. 'Don't think about it.'

'That's impossible.'

Neither of them spoke.

'It's like having a sickness you forget you have,' Amri described, 'but every now and then it rises up, and you feel ill.'

'But there's nothing you can do, man. I'm not going to say you have to move on, because it's hard, but you've got to keep pushing.'

Carl patted Amri on the back.

After a moment, Amri nodded.

'C'mon,' Carl said. 'Let's go.'

When Amri arrived home, he made something quick for him and Kali to eat. Afterwards, he descended into the basement. The table was covered with tools and various items he had bought in accordance with the instructions he had found online. He turned his laptop on and opened the link he had started visiting each evening. He was careful to keep the volume of the video low as the ex-ammunition technician in it explained each step, which he followed and repeated numerous times until he was sure that what he was making reflected exactly the version on the screen.

The following day, when Amri returned from work, he was surprised to find the house silent again with no trace of Kali's music. As he climbed the stairs, he caught a glimpse of Kali running from his room to hers. He continued up and checked his bedroom. She hadn't touched anything. He went back down the corridor and pushed his daughter's door open. She was sitting on her bed in her pyjamas, wearing her headphones and reading a magazine.

'It's 6pm. You're not planning on going to sleep now.'

Kali didn't move. Amri perched himself on the end of her bed and folded his arms. She pushed her headphones up leaving the strap of it above her forehead as if she was hiding behind them.

'What were you doing in my room?'

Kali stared into her lap. 'I was looking at the lines on your wall – I'm sorry.'

Amri found himself glaring at her and forced himself to relax. He noticed that her room seemed to have more space. 'You've thrown some things out?'

She nodded.

'I've given you a lot of money for those clothes, Kali. Don't—'

'Why do you do that?'

'Do what?'

'Count the days on your wall. I remember when I was a kid. Like really young—'

'You're young now.'

'And I remember you doing that, and Mum got so angry with you. Why are you doing it again?'

'They're building flats where Adea went missing,' Amri eventually said. 'It's reminded me that I'm the only one who remembers, and the lines help me not to forget.'

'Dad.' Kali paused, trying to count in her head but quickly gave up. 'What happens if you run out of space?'

'There'll always be space.'

'But why on the wall?'

'Because anything else I can hide or get rid of. I have to look at my wall every day.'

'It isn't normal.'

Amri shot Kali a sharp look and she flinched. He stood up. 'Don't keep those things on your ears for too long. You'll go deaf.'

He walked out and headed down into the basement.

'Do you know what my problem is?' said Carl. 'I live outside my means. I've been telling Stacey that she's going to have to cut back on the kids having so many extra activities. We can't afford it. It's frustrating.' He bit into his sandwich.

'I can imagine.'

'Sometimes I think I should've been like you, one child and no more.'

Amri nodded.

Carl stopped just before he was about to take another bite out of his sandwich. 'You good?'

'What? Yeah, I'm good.'

'Jesus, stop thinking about the park, man.'

Amri ignored him.

'I say that ... but I'd probably keep hope too if I was you.'

'You don't know if you would. People forget. Everyone forgets.'

Carl shook his head as he chewed.

Amri thought about the diggers churning up the soil in Hil Park and the steamrollers flattening everything beneath it. He pictured the bones of Adea being tumbled by the construction and shut his eyes to disintegrate the thought. 'I need to stop it,' he murmured, and only realised he'd spoken aloud when he saw Carl's profile.

'Stop what?'

'Nothing.'

'What? Tell me.'

'Just leave it.'

'Stop what, Amri?'

'I'm saying I need to stop it,' Amri shouted. 'The flats being built, the park being dug up.'

Carl laughed. 'Alright, chill ... You never know, they might find something when they bring it all up.'

'They won't.' Amri fell silent. When he spoke next, his voice was unsteady. 'I've been thinking of ways to stop the construction work.'

'Are you being serious?'

Amri remained facing forward and watching the cars pass on the road in front of them.

'Amri, your sister's gone. Do you know how many people went missing during the storm? How many lunatics used it as an opportunity to do twisted shit?'

He remained quiet.

'Exactly. Adea wasn't the only one. Other people have moved on. Do the same.'

He glanced at Carl.

'I'm sorry, but it's the—'

'What would you do?'

Carl straightened up in his seat. 'Twenty years is a long time. I wouldn't lose hope, but I wouldn't go about it the way you are right now. I'd get the media and the police involved. I'm not sure. If the worst did happen to her, maybe I'd save up and go to that Eden place, if it's even real. Find out that way.'

'We tried the media, we tried the police. My whole family endured that, and they found nothing. Not a clue, not even an idea about an idea. And I can't afford to go to Eden anyway.'

Carl turned away and frowned. 'Let's change the subject. You sound like a nutter.'

Amri leaned forward and started the truck.

'You have a daughter.'

'I thought you wanted to stop talking about it?'

'What was your idea? Cut at it with some shears? You had a stroke of madness just then. Check yourself.'

Amri didn't respond and instead began to pull out.

The following morning, Amri headed back to Hil Park. The construction had accelerated, and the sound of the men working was louder. The grating of the machines was now relentless, and the footpath beside the hoarding had few people walking it. Amri observed the area and saw most people were now travelling on the walkway opposite to escape the clamour. He turned his focus to the park and looked up; what had been a skeleton a few weeks ago was beginning to flesh out. He trod around the panels until he found one that was easiest to mount. He jumped up and grabbed the top edge of it before hoisting himself up so he could see over it. Much of the park had been dug up.

'Are you alright?' someone shouted.

Amri followed the voice and peered upwards. A man in a safety helmet was leaning out of a cabin crane and staring down at him. Amri dropped down, but the builder was high enough that he could still see him.

'I know people are eager to see what we're cooking up,' he shouted, 'but you'll have to wait. Health and safety.'

Amri didn't speak.

The man returned to his work. Amri took a few steps backwards and looked up again at the scaffolding.

The following day at work, he made arrangements to take two weeks off.

He spent that time in the basement. He started a pattern of waking and making breakfast for him and Kali, and then, when she left for school, going to his room and adding to the tally on his wall, before spending the hours Kali was away working on his explosives.

He tested them in the garden, and at the end of the first

week he achieved a successful detonation that made a car alarm go off. Encouraged by his success, he decided that at the end of the following week he would enter Hil Park and attach the charges to the foundations of the growing apartment block.

Carl rang Amri twice in the first week, and both times Amri ignored him. He rang again at the weekend, and Amri turned his phone off. On the Thursday of the second week, after Kali had returned from school, Amri was in the basement when he thought he heard a knock from upstairs. A minute later he heard Kali running down. She opened the basement door.

'Carl's here.'

Amri peered over the top of his laptop at her. 'Tell him to go. I'm busy.'

'What? Why? It's Carl. You could do with the company. You've been down here for days.'

'I'll be finished soon. Tell him I'll see him next week.'

Kali turned away and ran back up. A few seconds later, Amri heard footsteps that he knew didn't belong to Kali coming down the stairs. He lowered the tabs on his screen as the door opened slightly to reveal Carl peeping out of the gap.

'Kali told me to come down,' Carl announced as he stepped in. 'What's happening? I thought I'd come round. Hope you don't mind. You weren't picking up.'

Amri closed his laptop. He saw Carl's eyes scan the equipment on his table.

'What you making?'

'Nothing.'

'That's obviously not nothing.'

Carl's expression hardened as he inspected the pieces Amri had been working with.

'I'm trying to build a new kind of engine.'

'For what?'

'You're going to laugh.'

'I won't. Tell me.'

'For my lawnmower.'

Carl's frown faded. 'Jesus, looks like you've been working hard in here. You trying to revolutionise the industry or something?'

'Maybe.'

Carl studied the mess in front of him again. 'Doesn't look like an engine.'

'These are different parts. I'm trying to build components that'll give the mower more power but with barely any noise.'

'Oh. I see. That is revolutionary – a silent lawnmower.' Carl laughed. 'Wow. How come you didn't tell me about it?'

'It's just an idea. It's hard. I've barely managed anything close to what I'm trying to do.'

'Don't be hard on yourself. Give it time.'

Amri nodded. 'What's so urgent you had to come round anyway?'

Carl shook his head. 'Nothing really. Stacey wants to have a party for Max's birthday. Obviously she wants you and Kali to come. She's been stressing about confirming the numbers, that's why I was calling. She's taken over the house, to be honest. Any excuse to get out.'

Amri smiled. 'Let's go upstairs. I'll order some pizza.'

He stood up, and he saw Carl glance at the table again before heading back to the door.

When the weekend came, Amri didn't sleep well. He woke early on Sunday morning and was careful not to do anything that Kali might think was unusual. The hours lumbered, and he tried not to check the time on his phone or the clocks in the house. Kali's endless enthusiasm meant he could easily feign interest in what she was saying whenever she spoke to him by giving frequent nods and making brief comments, but he made sure to remain mentally preoccupied with what he planned to do that night. When late evening arrived, Amri found himself tapping the floor gently with his foot as he waited for Kali's bedroom light to go off. A few minutes after midnight, when Kali was finally asleep, he gathered his equipment and crept out of the house.

There was a closed café opposite the park. Amri was tucked into its boarded entrance, staring into the darkness. The silver of the steel from the site glinted underneath the moon. He walked forward a few steps, but before he crossed the road, he froze. His heart had started racing, to the point that it was making him shudder. He returned to the café doorway and remained there, wringing his hands together and taking deep breaths until it stopped.

He wasn't sure how much time had passed when he had finally gathered the courage to advance again, but when he did, the air felt chilled and biting. The moon was refusing to hide and glowed in a way that made him think something omnipresent was watching him. He reached the construction hoarding around the edge of the park and threw his rucksack over the top. It took him several attempts to climb the panel, and when he eventually managed to, he fell down and landed on his side. He caught his breath and staggered to his feet. He took his torch out. The dry grass crunched noisily beneath him as he neared one of the steel pillars, and as he was about to open his rucksack he hesitated; he was sure he had heard what sounded like rustling in the distance. He raised his torch and shone it in all directions. He scanned the parts of the park the light illuminated but saw no one. Holding the torch between his teeth to free up his hands, he gently pulled one of the explosives out of his bag. It was heavy and cold, and he could feel the tape around it as well as the unpleasant texture of the tied wires. He attached it to the metal. Despite the chill he was sweating. He heard the rustling again but was now certain it was being caused by footsteps over the grass that were getting louder and quicker.

He pulled the torch out of his mouth. 'Who's there?'

'Police!'

Lights blanketed Amri's vision as several armed officers raced towards him. He dropped his rucksack and sprinted. He stumbled over the uneven surface in the dark but pushed himself to his feet and trudged ahead. He fell again and could hear the men behind him nearing. When he risked a glance back over his shoulder, the multiple figures chasing him were obscured by the darkness and the flashing of torchlights. He struggled to his feet and lurched forwards before hitting the ground again. This time, as he pushed himself up, a cramp-like pain engulfed his entire body. He collapsed, trembling uncontrollably as the taser shocked him. By the time it finally stopped, he was shaking; the torchlight seemed painfully brighter, and as he rolled onto his back, the moon was not where he expected it to be – beyond the towering steel pillars – and seemed further away. There was shouting all around him, and he could taste mud in his mouth. He felt several hands grab hold of him and force him around before shoving his hands into cuffs.

CONSEQUENCES

Amri rubbed his eyes with his knuckles and blinked. The ceiling was white, and he could tell it was bright outside without having to look. His window was open slightly, allowing the breeze to gently move the curtains. It was quiet, save for a few distant voices belonging to the other inpatients, and when he eased out of bed and checked outside, he saw them wandering around the garden. A fly hit the window several times before buzzing away. Amri switched on the radio on his bedside table. The current station was playing modern pop, so he flicked through it until he found a station playing music from the late-2030s before lying back down. It wasn't time yet. He waited. Three-quarters of an hour passed before he checked the clock on the radio, and he allowed for a further fifteen minutes to wither before putting his clothes on: a plain T-shirt, jogging bottoms and trainers.

When he left his room, he told a staff member he was expecting visitors. He was taken down an airtight corridor, past a few offices, to an area reserved for guests. Kali and his ex-wife, Lorine, were sitting at a table. Kali smiled at him, but Lorine just stared. He pulled out a chair and sat.

Kali was wearing a baggy vest and a plain cap he'd expect someone like Carl to wear. It was the blandest outfit he had seen her in. Her nails weren't varnished, and her trainers were unmarked and without patterns. He felt like saying something but held off as it occurred to him that her lack of effort may have been due to his absence.

'How are you?' asked Lorine.

Amri was hunched forward slightly. 'I'm doing okay.'

No one spoke.

'The food is good,' he added. 'I'm talking to the other people here as well. It's peaceful.'

Lorine nodded. 'That's good.'

She bit her bottom lip, and they watched each other. Amri held his breath as he thought about holding onto her and apologising for what had happened. The longer he watched her the more he thought he saw affection in her study of him as well as sorrow.

Kali spoke. 'This isn't how I imagined—'

'Amri,' Lorine said, cutting Kali off. 'You'll finally get the help you need now, and you'll be better for it.'

Amri opened his mouth but his words wouldn't leave him. He held eye contact with her and gave her a weak smile.

'What were you going to say?' Amri asked Kali.

'It's not how I imagined it,' Kali answered. She eyed the room. 'It's so calm and quiet. Do you know when you're coming out?'

Lorine shot her daughter a disapproving look.

'It's okay. I'm not sure, but it'll be soon.' Amri shifted his focus to the corner of the room to give himself a moment away from the piercing eyes of his ex-wife and daughter. 'They say I'm getting better. That's all that matters.'

'How are they treating you?' said Lorine.

'The people are friendly. Almost too friendly, but they care.

I'm getting used to it – I'm seeing the benefits.'

Kali's expression fell and her lips curled downwards. 'Was there really something wrong with you then?'

Amri's eyes widened, and he leaned towards her. 'No. It's just that I'd lost a bit of focus ... Enough about this.' He smiled. 'How's school? Did you ever learn that tie?'

Kali was quiet. She clenched her fists. 'School's okay... and I did.'

'Did the other girls copy?'

Her face lit up a little. 'Two of them tried to, but they couldn't do it. They asked me to teach them, but they didn't have the patience. I'm learning a new one anyway. I want to learn them all.'

Amri forced a chuckle.

'Dad?'

'Yeah?'

Kali stared at her father. 'I'm sorry about letting Carl into the house that time. If I had known—'

'Kali,' Lorine snapped.

'It's alright.' Amri rested his elbows on his knees and leaned forward. 'Forget about that. It doesn't matter any more.'

Lorine breathed out. 'I told Kali not to talk about what happened, but ...' She shook her head. 'Seeing as she's brought it all up ... There was another article online about you.'

'What did it say?'

'More of the same. Mostly about the storm and the people who were never found.' Lorine held his gaze. 'But people do remember.'

'Okay... How's work?'

For the next half hour, Amri spoke to Lorine and Kali about everything but the treatment centre he was in. He teased and laughed, and the more cheerful Kali became the more he tried to keep his family's attention away from the residential home and from what had happened to bring him there.

By the time they were due to leave, the mood had lightened, and Kali asked him if there was anything else he needed from home.

'I've got everything.'

'Okay. I tried to bring your pictures from your bedroom, but Mum wouldn't let me.'

Lorine swatted Kali's shoulder. 'You talk too much.' She picked up her bag. 'Let's go.'

Before Lorine stood up, Amri reached across and touched her hand. 'Thank you for coming.'

Lorine squeezed his hand in return. She got to her feet and Amri joined her. She hugged him. Kali followed suit, slipping her arms around Amri as Lorine headed for the door. She held on for several seconds.

'Carl said he's sorry about everything.'

Amri was silent.

'Mum doesn't let me play loud music,' Kali said quietly, with her head pressed against his chest.

'Doesn't she?'

'Nope. That's why I wanted to stay with you; you're cooler than Mum.'

He chuckled.

'What are you saying?' Lorine shouted. 'C'mon, you'll see him again.'

Kali let go, and Amri felt her touch the pocket of his jogging bottoms as she did so. Lorine opened the door. Kali's brave expression failed as she turned and began walking out.

'I don't like that top,' Amri said. 'It's far too big.'

Kali halted. She grinned.

Amri watched the two of them disappear, and their figures were replaced by that of a worker who politely gestured for him to make his way out.

When Amri was back in his room and sitting on his bed, he felt something in his pocket. He reached inside and pulled out a photo. It was the picture of him and Adea that he'd had on his bedroom windowsill at home. He flipped it over and saw Kali's handwriting: *Mum wouldn't let me bring anything, but I brought this. I don't see what the problem is. As long as you don't forget about your sister, then that's all that matters. I know if I was missing, that's the only thing I'd care about. I wouldn't want people to forget about me. See you soon.*

Amri lay back on his bed. He stared at the ceiling and thought about his sister, flicking through the memories he still had of her, and marvelled at just how much Kali reminded him of her.

Room Four

David was sitting in his boxers. His windows were open wide, and dots of water animated the glass, but the air outside was warm and muggy and did little to cool his room. He had his phone to his ear and was listening to Leon trying to convince him to go on holiday.

'What do you mean you can't come?'

David pinched the bridge of his nose. 'I can't afford it.'

'So?'

'You're not listening; I haven't got the money.'

'Listen, you've got it. It's only a week. You won't need more than two thousand, max. Go into that magical pit of yours and make it happen.'

'The pit's empty.'

'It's never empty.'

'Leon, I can't afford it.'

'We're all going you know?'

'I know.'

'You'll regret it, man.'

'You think I don't know that?'

'Don't miss yourself then.'

'If I could come, I would.'

'David, shut up. Stop making excuses. Just come.'

David chuckled.

'Seriously, it won't be the same if you're not there.'

'It's summer here now, anyway.'

'You're joking?'

David looked through his window at the light but steady rain that fragmented the view of his garden, which was bare and unkempt. He could feel the hot air and smell the moisture of the falling water, and it created a sensation that made him think the earth was sweating. Leon continued to speak, and David wondered what it would be like to leave Crewchester in the summer and go to one of the places that was always advertised on TV, where weeks went by without the sun failing to show.

David swore under his breath. 'You guys are going to fucking ruin me ... I'll see what I can do.'

'Jesus, finally. I'll send you the details again. Let me know when you've got your ticket.'

'Okay, go away now.'

Leon laughed.

David ended the call. He stared at his window and noticed peeling paint around the frame. A strip of water from the drizzle outside had somehow entered and was running down the front of the glass, and he watched it for several moments before opening the Your Bank application on his phone. He booked a fifteen-minute appointment for the following afternoon in Room Four. Lifting his phone, he said, 'Turn off.' The screen darkened and the phone shut down.

A flag bearing the bank's logo was attached to the spire at the top, and it waved slowly in the hot air. The streets were busy, and David was forced to move slowly as he approached the building which had once been a church. Its exterior was now painted white, but it still had its Christian architecture.

Inside, the floor was marble, and the furniture was transparent. Opposite the meeting rooms on either side of the floor, customers were sitting on rows of see-through, cushionless chairs. David gazed up at the ceiling, which narrowed as it reached the base of the spire. It was so high that he felt dizzy once he looked back down. As he proceeded, some of the other visitors glanced back at him. No one was smiling, and there was little conversation. He reached the attendant, who was standing behind a tall white desk with two security guards on either side. Behind them, there were a few tables where other attendants were talking to account holders. Their interactions were short, and within a few minutes the customers were sent to sit and wait opposite the meeting rooms.

'I have an appointment with my account,' David said.

The attendant pressed a button on the surface of the desk and gestured for David to put his hand on the digital circle that appeared.

'You're in Room Four. There's someone in there, but they'll be out in a few minutes.'

'Thanks. I want to change the setting of my account from Critical Adviser to Impartial as well.'

'You can't do that here. You have to change settings with your account directly.'

David stared at the attendant. In response, the guards glared at him, which made him back away and search for a seat.

The passing minutes for David felt stretched, and he found himself glimpsing to his left and right, waiting for something to happen to help numb the feeling of time struggling to progress, but there was nothing but other people, like himself, sitting in silence. Eventually, he saw the door to one of the rooms open and a woman walk out who was rubbing her eyes with her wrist and holding her linen jacket in her other hand. As she hurried forward, she tripped over the trailing sleeve of her garment and collided with a chair. The bank fell silent. David waited for the woman to stand up, but she didn't. She remained bent over on the floor with her head in her hands. Two security guards ran towards her, and when the woman moved her hands from her face, David saw watery, black lines running from her eyeliner.

'I hate her,' the woman mumbled as one of the sturdier guards forced her to her feet. 'I swear to God I hate her.'

David looked away from her and at his feet as they ushered her out of the bank. He started tapping the floor with his foot. The door to Room Four opened, and a man came out. David peered into the colourless room as the door slowly started to close, before standing up, pulling it open and walking in.

Inside Room Four, it was dim. There was a screen with a hole beneath it on the wall to the right. David put his hand into it, and a message appeared asking him to enter his PIN. He pressed the keys gently and selected the option: SPEAK WITH YOUR ACCOUNT. Stepping back, he watched as a blue light appeared. It flickered, before becoming a hologram of a man in a V-neck jumper with a shirt and tie underneath. The hologram smiled at him.

'Good afternoon, Mr Kamara.'

'Hey.'

'I haven't seen you in some time. I hope you're well.'

'I'm good, thanks.'

'How may I help you?'

David didn't answer straight away, and when he did, he stuttered. 'I want to increase my overdraft.'

His account's eyes widened. The room was still lacking in light, and the blue glow from his account did little to illuminate it.

'You want to increase your overdraft?' David's account inspected him before stepping from its spot and circling him. 'You've been living off of your overdraft for eighteen months.' It stopped walking and faced him. 'I understand you may feel like you need the extra money now, but I strongly advise that you reconsider.'

David laughed. 'Don't worry, it's only temporary. I'll clear it and get in the black again.' The air inside the room felt stuffy as he waited for his account to reply, and the warmth made him fidget.

'I'd say otherwise. Given your history with money.'

David glanced at his account; he could have sworn it had smirked. It started drifting again with its arms crossed behind its back.

'It's my money, and I appreciate your advice, but like I said, I'm going to clear it. It's only—' David stopped. He was sure his account had chuckled.

'Is everything alright?' it said. 'Please, continue.'

David glared at it until it stopped moving. It smiled at him.

'It's only temporary,' he finished. 'I need to increase it, and

I'll sort it out eventually.' His account didn't speak, and he thought it was now looking past him, not at him.

'November eighteenth, 2049.'

'What?'

'On November eighteenth, 2049, Mr Kamara, you said: "I want to open an overdraft of five thousand pounds."'

David faltered as he heard the playback of his own voice.

'June third, 2050, you said: "I want to increase my overdraft to six thousand five hundred pounds. I'll sort it out in a couple of weeks." January fifth, 2051, you said—'

'Stop it!'

'And look where we are now, Mr Kamara.'

David opened his mouth but didn't trust himself to speak.

'Again, I advise you not to increase it, and to act with more prudence so that the overdraft is no longer your financial home.'

His account was now still as it waited for his response. It was exactly the same height and build as him and observed him in a way that he thought was unnatural. He looked to the floor. 'I need to pay for a holiday ... I can't let everyone down.'

'A holiday? When do you fly?'

'July thirteenth. I come back July twentieth.'

'Mr Kamara, that is an asinine idea.'

David raised his head and clenched his fists. 'I said I will. Now, increase it by a further two thousand pounds.'

'Are you sure, Mr Kamara? That will be the limit. You won't be able to increase it any more after this.' David didn't answer, and his account went on. 'Maybe you're just not capable of functioning well financially. That's what your pattern of actions tells me.'

'Increase my overdraft. Now.'

His account blinked back at him, expressionless. David wiped the sweat off his forehead. He felt the moisture on his fingertips and rubbed it on his shorts. He could hear the muffled sound of someone banging on the door.

'Do it,' he shouted.

'It's been done.'

David barged through his account towards the exit and pulled on the cold door handle.

'Mr Kamara, promise me that you'll make another appointment as soon as you get back, so that we can discuss how to get you out of this hole.'

David swore under his breath before wheeling around and reaching for the screen on the wall.

'Mr Kamara – David – please, you set me at Critical Adviser for a reason. Let me help you.'

'Be quiet.'

'Promise me, David, that you'll see me when you come back.'

'Change your setting to Impartial.'

David's account stood straight. 'Setting: Impartial. Will that be all, Mr Kamara?'

'Yes.'

'I hope you have a lovely day.'

David pulled his hand out of the slot and watched with unease as his account disappeared.

A woman with dishevelled hair and bags under her eyes was standing in front of the door when David emerged. 'About time,' she said. She brushed past him and entered Room Four, slamming the door behind her. David ignored the faces that were silently watching him. He headed towards the transparent water dispenser that was near the attendant's desk and filled a cup. He opened the message Leon had sent him, linking him to the flight he should book. After hesitating for a moment, he bought the ticket. He texted Leon, and Leon responded immediately: Yes! Just wait until you're somewhere that isn't caught in an eternal downpour. You'll thank me for bringing you to your senses.

David filled another cup and saw the sturdy security guard scrutinising him.

'You alright?' the guard questioned.

'I'm good.'

He took a sip of his water. A woman was discussing her account with an attendant in the space behind him: 'What other settings does my account have?' she asked.

David listened as the attendant explained.

'Okay,' the woman said, 'I'll change mine to a Critical Adviser then. I need someone to keep me in check.' She laughed.

David downed the cup of ice-cold water and walked out.

An Ill Wind

Carrying out company inspections, fitting smoke alarms and telling children why it was important not to call us about pets stuck in trees had become the bulk of our responsibilities. Most of us couldn't remember the last time we'd seen a fire, other than using a lighter to spark a cigarette or ignite a stubborn cooker hob.

When the public finally began to wonder why there were so few of our symbolic red trucks on the road, it arrived: The Constant Storm, The Tempest, The Fourteen Days of Hell, or whatever they wanted to call it.

Overnight, calls for inspections, smoke alarm installations and school presentations stopped as nature began playing a cruel game of tumbling towers with city skyscrapers and apartment blocks, using the increasing death toll as its score card. Retained firefighters were made whole time, the song of the fire truck returned, and our iconic siren – which neither the police nor the ambulance service could match, in melody or in decibel – cut through the shriek of the storm. People gathered and filmed whenever we arrived, and each drop of sweat that fell from our faces was recorded, documented and praised.

Fourteen days later, the public were told that there was no end predicted to the storm. People covered their mouths in shock as they watched their screens; children looked up at their parents, trying to understand what was wrong; workers hurried home; while supposed friends of our nation who were yet to be affected recited in rich detail how we were being torn apart, but how it was 'too dangerous' for them to lend a hand.

The same people who had progressively made us useless now reiterated how important we were.

We listened, and we worked every extra hour we were given.

Now, while the country tries to cope with life during the storm, we cross towns and cities fighting fire, saddened by the endless destruction of homes, jobs and lives, but never refusing the opportunity to bathe in media praise, to earn more and to experience the kind of security we had become unfamiliar with. Yet, all of this occurs alongside the pain of having to wake every morning unsure as to whether the blessing of the storm has come to an end.

Bonfire Hero

From the lamppost he was perched on, Christian was watching a woman get into the back seat of a car. An exploding firework shifted his attention to the sky. It was the first of the night he had seen, and it reminded him that it was Bonfire Night. He watched it force an eruption of colour into the darkness then returned to studying the people in the vehicle; the woman leaned forward and extended her hand while the driver reached behind him. Christian skulked to the end of the post before dropping off it, landing on all fours. He stood up, approached the car and tapped on the window. The driver lowered the glass, and the passenger beside him leaned over to see who was there. Before either of them had a chance to flinch after recognising who it was, Christian held the window down, causing the driver to jump back while the woman in the rear seat screamed. She got back out and ran. As Christian wrenched the car keys out of the ignition, he saw the passenger opening his door.

'Please don't,' he insisted. 'I don't want to chase you.'

The passenger stopped moving and slowly sat back in his seat.

'What do you want?' the driver asked.

Christian opened his hand.

The passenger shook his head. 'Are you joking?'

The driver shot his partner a frightened look. 'Give it to him.'

A quick and hushed exchange occurred between them, and Christian, who wasn't paying attention to their muttering, stood up straight and prepared to tear the driver-side door off but relented when he saw the passenger angrily reach back and pull a small bag from behind his seat. He shoved it at the driver, who couldn't hide his frustration as he carefully dropped it in Christian's palm.

The driver glared at Christian. 'Is that it?'

'The spliff too.'

The passenger put out the spliff he'd been smoking and handed it over.

Christian threw the keys into the car. The driver stared down at them and then glanced back up. Christian could feel the driver's eyes on him as he walked away.

There was silence. The car engine screamed, and the wheels screeched as the two men accelerated down the road, leaving behind the smell of burning rubber. Christian raised the bag so that it was at eye level, and he heated his hand up until it dissolved, turning the powder and pills into smoke, before letting what was left fall onto the road. He lifted his mask up and rubbed his face with his free hand. His fingers rippled over the burn on his right cheek. After checking to see if anyone was nearby, he brought the spliff he had confiscated to his mouth. He held the end of it with his thumb and index finger and felt it soften as he burned the end of it with his fingertips. The heat of the smoke stroked his face, and he could smell the musky scent of cannabis burning.

'Oh shit,' someone said.

Christian looked up; a man was watching him.

'Visionary. It's you. Wow.' The man studied him. 'What happened to your face? Is that … Is that weed?'

Christian squashed the spliff and pulled his mask down. The man stepped back, dropping his things and raising his hands. Christian swivelled round and leapt onto a protruding part of a nearby building before climbing around it until he was out of sight.

The clouds were riding the black of the sky, and the moon was absent. The only light was from below, and Christian gazed upwards at the darkness as he strolled across a wide and flat rooftop. With both hands he took his mask off before coming to a halt. He closed his eyes and breathed in. The sound of a police siren rang out, and he kept his eyes shut. It grew louder, and despite his attempts to not listen, the hissing of the radio entered his ears: *House ablaze on New Street*. He squeezed his mask as he forced an image of people struggling to escape a burning house out of his head and returned his hearing to normal. When the siren had become distant, he opened his eyes. The sky was now decorated by faraway fireworks, and the lights from lamp posts and fast-food restaurants gave the street a smudged glow. Christian took his phone out of the inside pocket of his outfit and checked his messages. He opened the conversation he had been having with Rihanna, while another police car approached with its siren blaring. He ignored it.

How's your night? he typed. He sent the message and stowed his phone away.

From where he was standing, he could see most of the city centre; below him, there was a main street with shops and a few bars and pubs. Several cars passed through it as revellers made their way deeper into the city for the night.

He heard someone at ground level towards the rear of the building shout, 'Where the hell is Charlie?'

Christian leaned over the roof edge and peered down. There was a car parked in the alleyway that separated the building he was on from the one next to it. One man was leaning on the front of the car bonnet with his arms folded. He wore a long coat and had a well-kept beard. Another man was moving about in an animated way; he had a large winter coat on with a high collar shirt and tie underneath it. He was chubby and had short hair.

'Let's go without him,' the chubby one said.

The bearded one glanced at his phone. 'We'll wait. I'm guessing he's trying to grab a bonfire-themed photo of Visionary.' The man shook his head. 'He needs another hobby. Photos of that poor man's superhero won't win him anything.'

Christian chuckled and surveyed the main street, which led further into the city centre. He focused his hearing; everything seemed peaceful. The chubby man's voice caught his attention.

'He's put Holmechester on the map, you know? He came out of the fire and burned crime to the ground. Give credit where it's due.'

'He's overrated,' the bearded one said, 'and that whole story's rubbish.' He spat on the pavement. 'I keep saying he's a government experiment gone awry.'

Christian felt his phone vibrate. He retrieved it from his pocket, seeing a message from Rihanna.

It's okay. I'm not doing much, just watching a movie. You?

His phone vibrated again. You're never free on Saturday nights anyway, so why are you asking? And it's Bonfire Night. Why aren't you out like normal people?

Because I'm working like normal people, he replied. And I'm watching the fireworks. You're one to talk, when you're at home watching a film.

Christian heard shouting; down on the street, a few teenagers were running out of a small twenty-four-hour shop. The owner ran after them but slowed down when he'd covered only a few metres. While trying to catch his breath, he pointed after them and shouted in anger before going back inside. Christian looked away and into the alleyway; he saw a homeless woman approaching the bearded man and his chubby friend. She asked them for change.

'Get a job,' the bearded one told her.

The woman shrank back and approached someone else on the main street, where she was rejected again. Christian pulled the neck of his suit down and scratched underneath his chin. He let out a sigh and ambled to the other side of the building, opposite the row of shops, and leaned over. The street was empty except for a man and two women who were all kissing in a corner. One of the women had her hand down the man's trousers. Christian checked his phone. There were no messages. He took several steps back before running forward and leaping over the alleyway onto the taller building opposite.

He killed time waiting for a reply from Rihanna by focusing his hearing and listening to people's conversations. After a few minutes, the sound of the chubby man raising his voice at his friend cut through his focus. They were still talking about him.

'We should be grateful. Visionary's changed things for the better, and he's the closest thing we have right now to a symbol of hope. People need that since the storm hit – people need a champion. Other cities would kill—'

Someone screamed.

Christian focused on the direction of the shouting; a man in a hood was brandishing a knife, threatening another man who was calmly facing him with his hands slightly up. The hooded man's partner shoved his arm down until he lowered the knife. She yelled for him to stop and for them to leave. The hooded one continued to swear at the man he'd tried to attack as his partner dragged him away by his arm.

'So Visionary's changed things, right?' the bearded man said in the alleyway.

His friend didn't answer.

Christian unlocked his phone and read Rihanna's newest message: How do you have time to talk if you're working? And shush, I'm going to watch the fireworks later.

He replied: I've had enough of work. You do know it's 11:30 pm? First day in weeks without rain and you're inside watching a movie.

He put his phone away and heard the bearded man in the alleyway speak again.

'Give me his powers and watch what I'd do with them.'

'Which is?'

'I don't know, but I'd use them differently.'

'You're full of it.'

Several howling voices cut through the night. Quickly, Christian headed to the edge of the building, swearing under his breath, and saw two large packs of teenagers running with fireworks in their hands or hiding behind cars as they set them off at each other. They barged down the street. He counted more than ten of them. Other people ran and hid in corners, standing aside as the two groups charged through. Fireworks collided with shop windows and cars, and two bystanders were hit. When the group realised they'd hurt someone, they stopped firing at each other and sprinted away down the street.

Christian studied one of the hurt civilians; he was holding his face while his friends tried to calm him. Police cars eventually appeared, and Christian looked on as other people gathered around those who had been hit.

'Jesus,' he heard the chubby man in the alleyway say. 'Jesus fucking Christ.'

He was still on the rooftop, watching the police ask bystanders questions about what had happened. His fists were clenched, and he observed the response of the emergency services without moving.

There were two ambulances and a fire engine now, as well as several police cars, which he thought was more than necessary, but he kept his attention on what was happening below until he saw that the two individuals who were injured were conscious. As the commotion calmed, he saw that they were hurt but not severely harmed. He breathed out and whispered to himself, 'Thank God.'

Christian tugged at his phone until it was out of his pocket then read Rihanna's latest text: You've said you've had enough a hundred times. Make your mind up. And 11:30's early for me.

He started his reply but stopped before sending it to watch the paramedics lift the injured into an ambulance. He returned to his phone and reread the message he had typed: I haven't. I've only told you a few times that some of the people I have to deal with piss me off. Sometimes it gets a bit much, but I've never said I feel like quitting.

Rihanna replied: Relax. You're a taxi driver, not a cop. And why don't you do something else then? Something with regular hours. Then you could spend more time with me.

That would be nice, he wrote. Every night is the same madness. There's no shortage of bastards out here, I'm telling you. I might finish early.

He didn't send the message. He looked out onto the main road then back into the alleyway.

The bearded man was staring into the street. 'This city's vicious.'

'And you wonder why we need Visionary?' the chubby one said. 'This place was – and still is – a death trap, but it's less so now.'

'Have you heard about how he pulls dudes out of their cars through the door window? The scarring it causes is horrific.'

The chubby one shook his head. 'I haven't heard about him doing that for a while. I'm going to call Charlie, anyway.' He pulled out his phone and brought it to his ear. He waited for a few moments. 'No answer.'

'Told you. He's looking for that lunatic.'

Christian crossed his arms and scrutinised his mask in his right hand. In the darkness it appeared as if it belonged to an executioner. When he heard the ambulances leaving the scene, he watched them disappear, then sent the message he had typed to Rihanna.

She replied: You complain, but I think you're too attached to it. Definitely more to it than you are to me. And it's a bizarre job to be attached to, Christian.

He glimpsed at the main street and saw another ambulance speed through. Its sirens drowned the noise of everything else. He focused his hearing and listened to the paramedics in the vehicle. 'Another damn shop set alight. I hate Bonfire Night in this city.'

His phone vibrated: And you're being serious, right?

Is that surprising?

No, it's not. I just can't imagine you quitting anything, but it's about time. You're always exhausted, and I'm surprised you find time to text. Finish early today and stay at mine.

Christian observed a torrent of fireworks. It lasted for longer than he expected, and he found the constant spectacular effects inspiring. When the illuminations ended, he messaged back: You're right. I'll let you know.

He jumped to the other end of the rooftop and noticed the beggar he had seen earlier. A man slid past her and went into a shop as she asked him for money. A minute later, he came out and handed her a leaflet.

'Call these guys,' the man said. 'They may be able to get you off the street.'

Before Christian could read Rihanna's reply, a fight erupted outside a chicken restaurant. He observed the altercation and was relieved to see people from both sides calming the dispute. Eventually, the groups settled, and Christian smiled. He heard the men's voices in the alleyway again. Their conversation had returned to Visionary.

'He's stagnant,' the chubby one said. 'I'll admit that.'

'He's more than that. He doesn't care any more. Check this,' the bearded one lowered his voice, 'word on the street is he's been letting criminals slide.'

'How do you know what the word on the street is?'

'Just listen; my daughter's friend's oldest brother was burgled a few weeks back. Visionary came just in time, but he didn't throw a punch or anything like that. Do you know what he said instead?'

The chubby one shook his head.

'"Put it back, mate."'

'What do you mean?'

'That's what he said: "Put it back, mate."'

'That's it?'

'That's it.'

Taxis cruising through the streets were appearing more frequently. They dropped off clubgoers, adding to the crowds of people already in search of excitement, and Christian, who was leaning forward on the building's edge and resting one arm on his knee, watched them. After a few moments, he checked his phone and read Rihanna's message: Wow, you agree with me? That's a first. Don't take too long to let me know if you decide to finish early. I still want to see the fireworks.

You're right. That is a first. I won't keep you waiting.

He stared up at the night and started to think about the warmth of Rihanna's home, but before he could visualise being beside her, he heard the voices of the two men. They were still speaking about him and had reached common ground.

'You're talking like he doesn't eat, sleep and shit,' the bearded one said. 'He probably has a girlfriend, hobbies – an addiction maybe. From what I know, being a superhero doesn't pay. He could be any guy riddled with debts and doubts.'

The chubby one laughed. 'True ... Remember when he first appeared? And how he used to tie criminals to fences and attach that manifesto to them?'

The bearded one smirked and nodded. 'What was it called again?'

'"The Vision: How I'm going to end crime in Holmechester and how you can help."'

'That was it. Everyone really thought that this one man was going to solve everything.'

'They did. He probably did too, until pricks like you ground him down.'

'What?'

'You're saying he's ordinary, right? So think about what all your hate does to his morale. Despite all he does, people like you have always discredited him, and still do.'

Christian, tired of hearing about himself, turned away from their conversation. He listened to the sound of car tyres licking the road and the waves of voices underneath the growl of the wind and the explosion of fireworks. He stood still, holding his mask. The sound of several kids riding down the main street on skateboards came into earshot. They were shouting and laughing as they made their way down the street. He checked his phone when he felt it buzz: Have you decided yet?

He stared at the message before tucking his phone away and rotating his mask around in his hands. It felt heavy. A barrage of fireworks interrupted the siren of an ambulance. He studied the front of his mask as he listened to a police car following the ambulance and wondered if anyone would miss it if he never wore it again. He closed his eyes and tuned in to the paramedic's conversation: 'Two shops set alight, several people burned and multiple bonfires out of control? What is this?'

'This is Bonfire Night in Holmechester.'

The warning sound of another police car emerged, this time not fading as the vehicle struggled to make its way through increasing traffic. Christian brushed his fingers over the burn on his face. He took his phone out and rolled it in his hand. After listening to the noise below him for several more moments he composed a message: I'm going to see it through. I guess I can't help wanting to make sure people get home safely.

He walked towards the end of the building and heard the

chubby man in the alleyway speak. 'You complain, but if you had powers like that surely you'd try to do something as well?'

The bearded man was leaning on the car and focusing on the direction in which the ambulance had gone. 'True,' he said. 'Shit, I'll give him that. At least he— Charlie!'

Charlie was jogging towards them. 'I know. I'm late.'

'You're more than late,' the chubby one said. 'Why have you got your camera?'

The bearded one pushed off from the car and opened the boot. 'Knew it. Leave it in there.'

'Thanks. Give me a minute.'

Christian's phone chimed. He read the message.

That's cute, but every time I think you've come to your senses … Okay, another time.

Ahead, Christian could see the lights of the police car and ambulance flickering. He lifted his mask and pulled it on. Beneath it, the smells and sounds of the city receded. Christian moved back several steps. He arched forward and burst into a sprint. As he ran, the wind filled his ears, and he quickened as he neared the siren of the last ambulance that had passed. He grinned as he jumped over the alleyway towards another building. A firework exploded while he was in mid-air, and a camera flashed.

Cold Expressions

Esther approached the bridge with her hands in her pockets and her head tucked into her scarf. Ahead of her, she saw a man wearing a T-shirt and jeans clutching the top of the rail and watching the road below. She gasped, realising what he was about to do as he lifted one leg and tried to climb over the barrier. As if sensing her alarm, the man hesitated and glanced in her direction. Esther dropped her stare to the pavement, but when she reached him she couldn't help looking up at him.

'Are you okay?'

The man mumbled something.

'What were you about to do?'

He chuckled to himself and shook his head. 'To think I tried to pick a time when no one would be here to see me.'

Esther smiled weakly. She noticed sweat patches around the armpits of his shirt. 'Sorry to interrupt.'

The cold didn't bother her now, and she took her hands out of her pockets and positioned herself so that she had a better view of his face. He turned away.

'If you're trying to do what I think you are, then you shouldn't. What's your name?'

'It doesn't matter.'

A gust of wind swept past, making Esther shield her face as pellets of water blew against her. She thought she heard the man say something else but couldn't tell over the noise of the wind. The sound of voices made her turn; a boy wearing a beanie and a girl with her hood up were at the other end of the bridge walking towards them, laughing. She turned back to the man and saw that he was lowering himself onto the other side of the barrier. Esther moved towards him, speaking calmly.

'Okay, don't tell me.' She smiled, knowing he wasn't looking but hoping it would show through her voice. She crossed her arms and peered over the rail and saw a car pass underneath the bridge. It dispersed the water on the road. 'Whatever you can't find here, I promise you that you won't find it down there ... Come back over. There's something or someone that wants you back on this side. I know it.'

'Maybe you're wrong,' the man answered, 'and no, there isn't.' He held onto the barrier without moving, while Esther stared at his back but was too scared to move closer. He adjusted the position of his feet slightly. 'I think you should go. I really don't want anyone to see this.'

'Jump!'

Esther spun to face the noise. The boy wearing a beanie had his hands shaped like a megaphone over his mouth.

Beside him, the girl shouted, 'Are you really going to do it?' She was holding the drawstrings of her hood and pulled them tighter so that it covered the top half of her face, leaving only her grin on show.

'If you're not going to help,' Esther said with restraint, 'then please go.' She returned her attention to the man, and the boy shouted again for him to jump.

'Don't listen,' she said. She leaned over the edge and

watched him. He resembled a grief-stricken sculpture. She wanted him to move or say something, but he did neither.

'Are you going to jump or what?' the girl shouted.

Esther looked back. 'Stop, please.'

'He's not going to jump,' the boy said. 'I don't even want to see him do it.' He laughed. 'But at the same time, I don't want to miss it if he does.' He glanced at Esther before returning his attention to the man. 'Don't be a pussy,' he shouted. 'Jump.'

'Stop it,' Esther yelled. 'Leave, and let me talk to him.'

The cold pierced Esther's awareness again, and she could feel it crawling along her skin. She watched the man's shirt blow against him in the wind. He had leaned around as much as he could from where he was standing and was looking at all of them. The boy and girl stopped shouting, and Esther studied him: his shoes were tattered, which made her feel a stab of sympathy for him. His jeans were baggy, emphasising his thin frame, and she squinted at the faded graphic on his shirt and at his unkempt beard. She felt a look of pity growing on her face as her stare reached his eyes. They were brown like hers. She locked her gaze with his. He jumped. Esther shielded her ears with both hands and stared at the place where the man had been standing, unable to hear the sound of him hitting the road.

Buddhatarium

Laurence peered around the living room. He could see the meditator in the corner, and through the net curtains, he saw the silhouette of someone in the garden made noticeable by the growing sunrise. He froze. They were walking in a circle, and he observed them as he bent forward and crept towards the door. He opened it. The figure outside was his wife, Kiara, ambling in a stunned state with her arms hanging by her sides. When she noticed him, she came to a stop. She sauntered towards him and hugged him. Laurence felt the coldness of her skin through his top.

'I wanted to come outside and watch the sunrise,' she said. 'I didn't want to wake you.'

Laurence stared at her as she gazed up at him, and underneath his hands she felt delicate. Her face had a tranquil expression.

'Holkavta's the best investment we ever made,' she added.

He noticed her emphasis on 'we,' and realised she was happy, happier than he'd seen her for several years, but her posture was slack, and her eyes were only half-open.

'You've never been fussed about the sunrise before. Why now?'

'Because of Holkavta, of course.'

'What?'

'You don't know?'

'Know what? Please, fill me in. I'm struggling here.'

'Holkavta's powers are strongest during this time of day. I wanted to be near him, but outside so I could really feel it … feel it on my skin and—'

Laurence let go of her. He went back into the living room and then into the passageway, where he pulled the biggest of his daughter's hockey sticks from underneath the staircase.

'People need peace. Each and every one of us needs it, and I don't mean this in the same vein as us needing to breathe or eat – no. Peace, tranquillity, calm, are things we search for – the same way we search for a partner – from the moment we are born. That is why people buy meditators. They are … one thing in this world that can give us the calm we need and at the same time improve our spiritual fitness.'

– Xuewei Fang, chief executive of Buddhatarium

He should have been at work, and his daughter, Leona, at school, but instead, Laurence was behind the steering wheel while Leona was in the passenger seat. As his daughter spoke he nodded, mumbling a few words every so often to give her the impression he was listening, but he was thinking only of how long it was taking to get to Crewchester and then on to Buddhatarium, and how few hours he had left until Kiara returned home. Leona said something about her hockey practice, and Laurence grunted in reply.

'Dad?'

He was focusing on the road ahead.

'Does Mum know where you're going?'

He glanced at her; her large eyes were fixed on him. 'Of course she does.'

As he drove, Laurence thought about the events that had created what was happening now; a row had arisen between him and Kiara over whether they should use part of their savings to improve their home or keep it all for Leona's future. He was against it, but Kiara argued that their house was old and weather-beaten and needed external work. He had marched out of their bedroom the moment they had begun shouting at each other, and as he made his way downstairs, a still yelling Kiara followed. While her parents argued, Leona had climbed onto the kitchen tabletop and tried to reach the sweets that her mum had placed on top of the highest shelf. She persevered despite hearing the descending footsteps of her parents, and, realising she might not get it in time, she reached further than she would usually risk. When Laurence entered the kitchen with Kiara in pursuit, Leona froze at the sight of her raging parents. On Leona's face was an expression Laurence had never seen before, and he realised it was one she had never shown because she had never captured her parents being so hostile, and it reminded him just how well the two of them had been hiding it over the years. Then Leona lost her balance. Laurence could no longer hear Kiara's words as Leona fell back. He lunged forward. She crashed to the floor, bringing down with her a box of chocolates that burst open upon hitting the ground. When Laurence scrambled down to his hands and knees to check if she was okay, he saw in her frantic glances that she was more concerned with what was happening between her mother and father than her twisted ankle. Now, as he neared Buddhatarium, Laurence no longer held any qualms about lying to his wife and taking their daughter with him; just her presence had reinforced his confidence in his decision and stopped him turning back.

> 'For me, buying the meditator wasn't a last resort, but you know when your life has an empty space and you've done everything possible to try and fill it? It's the meditator that filled it for me. I'm no longer searching for the meaning any more; it's downstairs in my basement.'
>
> – Krista Kind, meditator owner

When they reached Crewchester, they headed straight to Buddhatarium. No breaks. Laurence parked the car once they were there, and the two of them made their way to the entrance. The building was mainly glass, and a few shop assistants were standing outside and greeting customers with a smile. Laurence felt himself relax, and he walked forward with Leona beside him. Inside was warm, and the air was fragranced with something sweet that neither of them recognised.

Meditators sitting upon giant stools with cushions on top made up most of the displays, while staff moved about in shirts bearing the popular image of a Buddhist praying. There was no music playing, and the sound of people cheerfully speaking and giggling filled the shop floor.

The meditators would have looked like regular people, had it not been for their shaven heads and the position they were seated in: legs crossed, forearms resting on their thighs, with their hands gently placed together and pointing upwards. They were clothed in silk robes and sandals. Laurence and Leona leaned forward to read the details on the front of a large stool that listed information about the meditator sitting on top of it: all of them had reached a state of peace and possessed an affinity with their souls. The age at which the meditator had achieved total purification was also displayed, which informed customers on the depth of experience it had within the four divine dwelling places of friendliness, compassion, sympathy and equanimity. Laurence had decided it would be better for his and Kiara's relationship, and in turn Leona's well-being, if he used part of their savings to buy a meditator that had reached nirvana, a perfect state of happiness, and had been familiar with it for at least a decade. He thought back to the videos he had watched, the FAQs he had seen, and the articles he had read that explained why couples who bought meditators went on to enjoy longer and better relationships – no longer plagued with many of the issues that others endured, such as emotional distance and inactive sex lives. The latter was something Laurence had tried not to think about since he and Kiara had stopped sleeping together, but as the idea of having a meditator had begun to grow in his mind, so had the memory of the attributes he had lost in his relationship.

The two of them browsed for over an hour, stopping once

to ask if there was anything else they should know in addition to the details given on the stools. A sales assistant told them that the amount of energy a meditator needed depended on its experience with the four divine dwelling places. The assistants worked slowly, wearing grins, and Laurence found he had a level of patience that he had never possessed before as he listened to them. He realised that Leona was calmer too. The two of them were at the end of the centre row when Laurence spotted a meditator at the furthest corner of the store. It was in red and brown robes, and from its pleased expression Laurence got the impression that it was still connected with reality, unlike the others, who appeared to be indifferent to the admiration of the customers around them, which made Laurence think they were lost in a spiritual state. His daughter picked up on this too, and as he began to saunter towards it, Leona hopped in front of him and pulled him forward, turning his slow pace into a jog. A few people were already eyeing the meditator when they reached it, and the two of them inspected its features. Its name was Holkavta. It had spent seventeen years in nirvana, reached the apex of self-purification and obtained the perfect disposition. The price tag was twenty thousand pounds, and it had a guarantee of fifty years before its field of serenity began to wear.

'Holkavta,' Laurence said to himself. 'Laurence, Kiara, Leona and Holkavta …' He inspected Holkavta again then scanned for a member of staff. When one appeared, Laurence gestured at them then pointed at the meditator. 'I want this one.' He heard Leona cheer behind him.

The store assistant nodded. 'Come this way.'

As they followed, the assistant told them about the different payment plans there were, and as he led them to a meeting room, Laurence noticed meditators he hadn't seen yet, which were unnaturally big. He couldn't stop his gawking as he passed one that was as wide as the three of them standing abreast.

'Ones like that,' the assistant said, 'companies buy for their office spaces. Or they're what the more well-off buy for their mansions.'

He nodded. The assistant continued to reel off terms and conditions as well as different payment options. When he repeated that the most common method of payment was in instalments, Laurence came to a halt.

'No. I'm paying it all now. In one transaction.'

The assistant's eyes widened. 'Are you sure?'

'I am.'

'As you wish.'

They followed him into the room. He closed the door after they entered and indicated for them to sit down. Once they had taken a seat, he brought out a multi-page form and laid it on the table. 'Fill in the first page for now. I'll talk you through the rest.'

Laurence started to write. The assistant asked him to turn the page then fell silent as Laurence read the rest of it. 'No returns or exchanges?'

'No.'

'Okay.' He returned to the paperwork. He began tapping the pen gently against the sheets as he thought about whether or not he should continue despite not being able to bring back such an expensive purchase – even if he got home and discovered Holkavta wasn't as effective as he had hoped. He put the pen down.

'Is everything okay, sir?'

He didn't answer.

The assistant leaned closer. 'Free yourself of doubt. The meditator will change your life.'

Laurence stared into the assistant's unblinking eyes. 'That's what I want it to do. That's why I'm here.'

'Then, if you truly feel that you need one, shall we continue?'

Laurence went through the pages of the form again, and he wondered how many more times he and Kiara would argue before one of them finally packed up and left. 'I don't just need one,' he said, lifting the pen. The air around him felt colder now, and in the corner of his eye he noticed Leona staring up at him. 'It's the only thing that'll put my house in order.'

The assistant beamed. 'That it will ... They're magical.'

Laurence felt a grin tugging at the corner of his mouth during the return journey to Holmefield, while Leona was gazing out of the car in a dream-like state. They drove slowly, irritating the drivers behind them. In the back seat was their new meditator.

They arrived home and accompanied Holkavta into the house before setting up the giant stool with a large cushion on top in the corner of the living room. Holkavta sat on it once they had finished and assumed a meditating position.

The two of them stared at it for a few minutes. Then, feeling restful, Laurence switched on the television.

As they both watched it, they became unusually transfixed by the images and didn't notice that the volume needed to be turned up.

They hadn't moved from in front of the TV when several moments later someone started knocking. Laurence got up and slowly made his way to the door. He opened it.

Kiara was rummaging through her bag. 'I think I left my—' She peered through the passageway into the living room, and her eyes fell on Holkavta. 'What the hell is that?' She pushed past Laurence. She noticed Leona, who was sunk into the sofa and wearing a blissful expression, then cast a glance at Holkavta before narrowing her eyes at Laurence, who was strolling towards her. 'How much?'

'Half of our savings.'

Kiara's jaw fell. She whispered, 'In instalments I hope?'

'In full.'

'In full?'

'You heard me the first time.'

'Did you at least speak with our account first?'

Laurence shook his head.

Leona was laughing now, and Kiara's eyes flicked back to her. 'Shut up.' She dropped her things and faced Laurence. 'What's wrong with you?'

Laurence waited for her to say something more, but she remained in front of him. He didn't break eye contact, and after a few more seconds of them standing off, Kiara spun around. She looked up at the ceiling and exhaled loudly until her voice rumbled and began to sound like a growl. She brought her hands to her face, and Laurence calmly waited for her to speak.

'Why did I marry him?' she hissed to herself. She pulled her hands down until they were resting over her mouth. 'I have every right to be angry with you.'

Laurence thought about replying but realised his new-found calmness left him undisturbed by Kiara's anger.

She swore under her breath and scrutinised Holkavta. Her breathing slowed and her posture relaxed as she focused on the meditator.

'But it's here now,' she said, 'so it doesn't matter any more, does it?'

Laurence tried to read her expression, but she was facing away from him.

She turned to him and sighed. 'Come on … Let's make something to eat.'

Laurence caught a glimpse of Holkavta; the meditator eyes were shut. Kiara's hand was now wrapped around his, and he felt her squeeze it lightly as she led him into the kitchen.

'My meditator wasn't exactly what I was expecting.'
'How so?'
'I mean, it met my expectations, and the effects it had on my family were therapeutic – constantly therapeutic, and that's what I never predicted; just how numb my household would become, but we were happier, so I guess I got my money's worth.'
– Mohamed Mahmood, meditator owner, taken from an interview with Steve Maillot on *The Maillot Show*

In the hours after Kiara came home to Holkavta, and in the following days and weeks, Laurence expected her to find time to express how upset she was with him, but this didn't happen in the way he imagined.

During that first evening, Kiara had become quiet, and at night in bed, she watched him for long periods before finally leaning over and kissing him. The act was something he had become unfamiliar with.

'We're going to speak about this tomorrow,' she said.

He thought about telling her to discuss it now, but didn't feel the urge to act on it, and he attributed this lack of forwardness to Holkavta.

The next morning, Kiara made herself a cup of coffee and sat in the living room staring at the meditator. When Laurence approached her, she smiled and gestured for him to sit beside her. She rested a hand on his knee once he had done so then returned her focus to Holkavta. Her smile decreased, and her slight movements over the settee as she adjusted her position so that both her legs were on the chair filled the silence.

'About the expensive purchase you made.'

She stopped. Laurence waited for her to continue, and she chuckled.

'There's something about it that ... I don't know, Laurence ... I don't, but ...' She studied the meditator. 'Amazing ... You're unbelievable.'

Laurence tilted slightly, as if wanting to create distance between himself and Kiara's unusually relaxed demeanour. She leaned across and hugged him, before letting go and yawning.

'It's done now. Let's just hope it's worth it.' She stood up and was about to leave the living room, but then said, 'You're taking Leona to school today, right?'

Laurence sat up straighter. 'I thought you were dropping her off on your way to work?'

'Not any more. I'm staying at home today. Going to call in sick. I need to relax and take everything in; reset myself.'

Laurence watched Kiara go. He turned to the meditator and tried to spot if there was something more to it other than what had been listed about its calming abilities, but he saw only its fixed posture. He leaned closer; the air around it had no smell, only an aura of purity. After what felt like no more than a few seconds, he realised he had been watching Holkavta for far longer than he thought when he heard Leona running downstairs saying she was ready to go.

As the days passed, news of Holkavta spread, and when Laurence and Kiara's neighbours asked if they could see it, the two of them were happy for people to come inside and share the experience. Laurence enjoyed watching the excitement they had before entering the house turn into a peaceful interest as they approached the meditator. He would offer them food and drinks, and once they had spent a bit of time inspecting the meditator and asking questions about it, Laurence would show them the way out. Most of them would then say to him, 'That's money well spent. You and Kiara have got it figured out.' They spoke in a near whisper, as if they didn't want Kiara to hear, despite her being in earshot. Laurence would smile at them, and after he had closed the door he would see Kiara behind him wearing a satisfied look. 'You were right,' she would say. 'It's what we needed.' He would then walk towards her and hug her.

Not long after buying the meditator, Laurence started to find life outside of home unrestful. Each day he would notice more and more that people had their worries and troubles etched into their faces. At work, this caused him to attempt to cheer people up, but this act was short-lived as many of his colleagues found this to be out of character for him. He got the impression that they thought he had become weird. On a few occasions they bluntly said that he was only talking like a motivational speaker because his life was now good due to the meditator. They seemed to resent his new character. He knew the rest of his family were going through the same experience without having to ask them, as they were all spending more time at the house than they had before. Leona was no longer hanging around with her friends after school and was now rushing home, and Laurence still couldn't get used to Kiara embracing him with a kiss whenever he returned home on a day where she hadn't left for work. Now, they had sex often, but it was patient, and, at times, Laurence found it lasted for far too long; he woke up in the mornings exhausted. As Kiara had decided she would now go to work only when she felt like it, she would spend those days lying in bed, leaving Laurence no choice but to head to the office. He wanted to tell her the toll such days were having on him, but he held his tongue so as not to risk interfering with her new level of bliss. He was becoming certain that the meditator had had a more profound effect on her than it had on him or Leona, but when he found out that his daughter had been just as badly affected as her mother, he began to question his decision to buy it.

Laurence was returning from work after an early finish. When he arrived home and opened the front door, he saw Leona midway up the stairs glancing back at him in her school uniform.

'Did school finish early?'

Leona didn't move.

'Hey? You alright?'

'I'm fine. Everything's fine'

'What are you doing home then? You shouldn't be in the house all by yourself.'

Laurence waited for a response, and his temper sparked when he was met only with his daughter's blank expression. He stormed into the living room with Leona running after him. On the seat closest to Holkavta was Leona's backpack. His daughter's voice chimed behind him.

'It wasn't so I could be near it.'

Laurence glowered at her, and she fell silent. He pointed towards the door and she walked out with her head down.

He glared at Holkavta and was for the first time completely aware of its pacifying effects as he felt his rising emotions being calmed. The sensation was akin to someone pushing him down gently as he tried to stand up. Not wanting to be dulled out of his irritated state, he forced himself around and trudged towards the front door, where Leona was waiting outside. He took her by her hand and pulled her to the car.

During the drive to Leona's school Laurence didn't speak, except for once: 'No hockey for a month.'

When they arrived, he found his daughter's teacher, Lucee.

He explained in detail what had happened. Leona's teacher told him that this wasn't the first time she had bunked school, and upon hearing that he glared at his daughter, who was staring at the floor. Her teacher took him to one side.

'They're a double-edged sword,' she said.

Laurence didn't answer.

She continued. 'A lot of people grow to dislike them, because they're the thing that makes everyone in their homes happy, rather than their own hard work … I mean, a bald dude sitting on a cushion who says and does nothing fixes all of your problems? Maddening, don't you think?'

'You sound like you've had one before.'

'My uncle did.'

'What happened?'

Leona's teacher gritted her teeth and then sighed. 'He wasn't the same, that's what. He'd made a fortune over the years, and not in the best way, and that played on his conscience, so in his later years he thought a meditator would help put him at ease.'

'Did it?'

She shook her head. Before speaking again, her eyes flicked to her left and right as if to make sure no one was eavesdropping. After seeing no one else was near them, she lowered her voice. 'Let's just say I preferred him when he was a criminal on the run than when he was wasting away, snorting coke beside his meditator.'

Laurence, stunned, tried to think of a reply, but the school bell rang before he was able to.

Lucee checked the clock. 'Anyway, what I'm trying to say is that I completely understand, and Leona's performance has been amazing this term, so her truancy hasn't affected her achievement yet. But no more of it, please.'

She gestured for Leona to follow her back to class.

Later that afternoon, Laurence explained to Kiara what had happened. He waited for her to reply, and she said, almost casually, 'She's said she won't do it again – and I believe her. She's only ten, after all. If she does it one more time we'll take her house keys off her. Simple. Relax.'

His wife was staring at Holkavta, unmoving. He briefly considered telling her the thoughts he had had about the meditator, but as soon as it crossed his mind he felt like he needed to sit down for a moment, so he did. Kiara leaned against him, and he kissed her.

'That was sweet, wasn't it?' she whispered. 'Have you noticed that?'

'What?'

'How everything is better ... Why did we ever stop loving each other like this to begin with?'

'I don't know. Why did we?

'Why did you leave the company you and your family had built for over a century?'

'Because when you hear about something for so long – nothing but good things – or when you are inside the ride for so long, in a car that has travelled around the world, when you finally come out of it and see for yourself what everyone has been talking about, what your family has educated you so much about – despite them never having the chance to see the car itself when it was in the city, the roughness and artificial structure of modern life – you realise that maybe the ride looks better in its place of origin, that your family and home have been telling you how good it looks because they understand where it comes from, the terrain it was designed for, but now it is somewhere else, and there are too many people around it, so you can't take it home. That's why I left. Meditators are for those who live outside, for people on a journey who need a place of peace before continuing – not for twenty-four-seven consumption – and I think this is the error that the West, and then the rest of us, made. After so many years dealing with the storm, we were too desperate to recreate the calmness before it, and this is why so many owners are experiencing the problems they are having now.'

   – Xuewei Fang, from an interview
     with *East Enquiry*

From under the stairs in the passageway, Laurence pulled the biggest hockey stick out of Leona's sports bag. Kiara had followed him inside from the garden. She was confused, and for a moment he felt himself faltering, then he remembered the shock of waking up to find the bed beside him empty and the disturbing sight of her wandering aimlessly in circles on the lawn. He looked into her eyes; they were unnaturally dilated. He raised the hockey stick. 'No returns or exchanges.'

He shoved past her and barged into the living room. He ignored her gasp and swung for Holkavta's head. Kiara shouted, jumping in front of the meditator, and the end of the stick struck her arm. Laurence threw his makeshift weapon aside, and Kiara grabbed onto the curtains as she stumbled, pulling them apart and revealing the rising sun. Laurence tried to hold her, but she fell before he could catch her.

'No,' she yelled.

Before Laurence could speak, she grabbed him. 'Come here,' she ordered, and started pulling him down onto the floor with her. 'Stop fighting it. This was what you wanted, wasn't it?'

'What—?'

'We're happy now. You just don't realise it yet.' She tugged at him again. 'Lie at his feet with me, Laurence. You'll feel it even more, and then you'll understand.'

Laurence lowered himself a little, and for a second time he felt the effect of the meditator clearly as his energy and panic began to deplete. He tried to support himself with his hands, balancing on one knee as Kiara continued to try and drag him down. 'Kiara, I'm sorry. I didn't—'

'You should be. That's going to bruise – badly … I can't believe you hit me.'

Before Laurence could apologise, Kiara shook her head. 'I know.'

He was about to get up, and she yanked him back down until he was lying on the floor with her at the base of Holkavta's stool. She held onto him, and he stopped struggling. 'I was aiming for Holkavta.'

'I know you were … but if it was me before, the old me I mean, then maybe you should've been aiming for me anyway.'

'No—'

'Don't defend how I was. I was difficult.'

Laurence felt his wife's grip on him tighten and her feet dig into him. Her fingers and toes were cold. 'I wasn't reasonable back then. I don't know why. I … It was just … I was just unhappy.'

Laurence thought he could hear light steps coming down the stairs.

'I felt like "Is this it? Is this really it for me?" I remember the past being so exciting, but what my life had become wasn't. But the meditator, Laurence, the peace it brings … It's made everything clear; the past wasn't so great either. Sometimes nostalgia is deception.' She stared at him. 'If you had killed it, that's what you would've taken us back to, the past, and it wasn't better. And yes, my arm is hurting.'

'Mum, Dad?'

Laurence and Kiara turned their attention to their daughter, who was approaching them.

'What was that noise?'

Before either of them could say anything, Leona crouched down and spread herself across her parents in a starfish position before trying to hug both of them at the same time.

Kiara's eyes returned to Laurence's. 'Let's keep it. Please?'

Laurence looked away and focused upwards on Holkavta, who appeared clearer in the still-growing sunlight. 'This is different,' he said quietly.

'This is what different feels like.'

'But it isn't how I imagined it.'

'But this is it.'

'What are you two talking about?' Leona said.

Leona appeared contented, and Kiara was now smiling with her eyes closed. She bit her lip as her daughter shuffled around and knocked her hurt arm.

'I'm so comfortable,' Leona added.

Kiara squeezed Laurence's hand. 'We're keeping it.'

Laurence shut his eyes and allowed Holkavta's aura to calm him further. When he opened them, he gazed at his wife and daughter and sighed. Leona giggled, and Kiara's smile hadn't faded. Leona asked her mum if she could bring more of her friends over to see Holkavta, and while they discussed it, Laurence closed his eyes once more and listened to their voices while ignoring the thin layer of sadness he felt and Holkavta's efforts to try and rid him of it.

The Weatherman

You said I was becoming senile.

It shocked and angered me, but I didn't argue.

On the surface, my life met all the requirements for such an assessment. I had stopped leaving the house; rent arrears that I had refused to ask for help with were becoming insurmountable; I was weaker, slower, lonelier, and if I had ever gone to my own mother's house after months without seeing her, and found her in the living room staring into the garden, and realised she hadn't moved for hours, I would've been worried too, but you were better than worried: you were proactive, which is to be expected given that you're a weatherman; prediction is what you're all about. I remember how you put your hand on my shoulder when you said it and how you lowered yourself until your eyes were level with mine. You didn't have to say anything more – I agreed with you. But on the flipside, Fabien, you had stopped coming to see me. It was gradual, as if you were conditioning me for this moment, so that by the time you visited that day, and despite me being able to manage without much help and too stubborn to accept the mantle 'old', I was lonely and defeated.

You placed a brochure in my lap and showed me its contents like you were reading a story to a child. 'Here,' you said. 'It's perfect for you. Paid for by yours truly.' You smiled. 'You'll like it,' you added. 'Forget about this place. It's empty and riddled with debt. Let the council have it.' I shut my eyes, and you patted me gently on the back. But despite this intervention, I didn't go into the home straight away.

I read the brochure every day after your visit and tried to dismiss it, but I was alone again, and you know me, Fabien, you know I was too proud to call you and ask for your company, and that I was too hard-headed to admit that the loneliness was killing me. I reread the one part of the brochure that kept picking at me: *Our sheltered housing doesn't remove your independence. What we offer is a community.* It was that word 'community' that I couldn't ignore. I crumpled the brochure and sat there cursing your name. You had backed me into a corner, and you had done it in such a way that I couldn't accuse you of doing so. That's what angered me. Eventually, hissing all of those expletives at an absent you became exhausting. The living room fell silent, again, and I was alone, again.

More time passed.

I wiped my eyes. I used both hands to lift myself off the chair so as to not strain my back. I lumbered to the phone and called the number on the brochure.

The next time I saw you, it was on the news during the early days of the storm. You had moved from regional to national. I was proud. Months had passed since I'd entered sheltered housing, but I'd yet to hear from you. Still, I was hopeful that you were going to come and visit at some point. I was sitting in a communal room surrounded by other service users.

That's what they called us, but I was nothing like them. Some of them would insist on reading the paper, only to forget what they had read by the time they reached the next page, so as you can imagine, Fabien, I hated being around them. There were some who had been there aeons, who had become sort-of leaders of the decrepit, and who thought they were experienced with new and less sociable users, like me. The two of us have never liked people like that, have we? I did like you used to tell me: *Give them bits of yourself. Just enough so that they think you're approachable.* That sorted everything.

When the storm finally arrived it was monstrous, but seeing you reassure everyone on television made it feel like nothing. I turned to Marc, a service user I could stomach because he talked little and listened lots, and said, 'That's my son.'

You looked great: clean suit, flawless hair and perfect teeth. Compared to you, the other presenters were sloppy, the women too concerned about their bust and the length of their skirts to have mastered good presenting, and the men unable to help looking like teachers. You should've have given them tips.

When you told the nation there would be no end to the storm, my first response was to remain optimistic. It was you giving the news after all, but as I watched you I noticed how you weren't fazed by the development; you only stuttered and wiped your brow, whereas for every other presenter on every other channel, calmness quickly gave way to fear. It struck me. My smile crumbled. How could someone be unperturbed about a storm that would kill thousands more than it already had and ruin the lives of countless others? As I watched your mouth move I came to an understanding: you weren't just antisocial, like I was; no. You were malicious; you were a misanthrope.

You continued to relay the bad news, and the communal area descended into hysteria. I looked around, becoming more and more frustrated with the impotent people surrounding me and with the looming noise of the storm. I started asking myself why I was here. I focused on you to take my attention off what was happening around me, but rather than calm me, your indifference to the situation irritated me further, and I thought: if you had continued to visit me, would I still have given up, surrendered my home and came here?

Your forecast ended, and the storm expanded into something much worse than we'd experienced in the past two weeks. I'd never seen anything like it. I watched it twist and grow, and as jagged strips of light stabbed the ground, I decided I was going to leave this place and pay you a visit.

Being more functional than the other walking corpses in the community, I had the presence of mind to go to my accommodation before the warden had a chance to advise me not to, which gave me time to pack some things into a bag without anyone peeking over my shoulder. I waited for night to fall, and as the hours passed the storm broke windows and knocked the electricity out. The warden, who was a nice enough man, braved the weather and went around each home telling everyone it was going to be alright. Only an idiot would have believed him. Soon after midnight, when everyone was in bed, I left my bungalow and started my journey.

I had only walked several metres when I had to stop and rest on my umbrella. Realising I would struggle to make it on foot, I used my dated mobile phone to call for help, but it wasn't due to my back pain, Fabien. Anyone would have struggled in those winds.

I've never been more grateful for those who are too avaricious to know the meaning of a work-life balance as I was that night. When the taxi arrived, I was holding onto a lamp post to keep myself from falling over. The driver jumped out and helped me into the car, and I winced as a sharp pain shot through my back.

'Why are you out here?' he said.

'I could ask you the same thing.'

He laughed. I told him to take me to the station, where I planned to wait until the first train to Denttingham arrived.

We spoke as he drove. His name was Alan, and he had a wife and two kids he'd do anything for.

'Even if it means killing yourself in this storm?' I commented.

He didn't answer.

I thought about you in the taxi, and I wondered how you were coping with the weather and if you had thought about me. I was more fascinated by the storm than afraid of it, but

Alan seemed nervous and kept talking. Several minutes into the drive we saw a car which had been flipped over. Then another. And another. Alan lost his nerve.

'Sorry, love, I'm not going any further. I'll drop you outside a bed and breakfast.'

By the time we reached one that had its lights on, he was sweating. He parked then told me the fare. I didn't have the money to waste. I rummaged through my bag and acted as if I had lost my purse. I gaped at Alan, horror on my face.

'We need to go back.'

He was silent for a moment. 'Get out.'

The second my feet reached the pavement, Alan did a one-eighty turn and screeched off.

It was a struggle to open the door to the B&B against the wind. When I finally did, I saw several people huddled together. Most looked like regular street furniture, but others had clearly just been unlucky. I could tell the owners were the couple standing behind the bar. They were tired, and they barely glanced at me as I found a corner in which to spend the night.

In the morning, the weather calmed slightly, so I made my way to the station, refusing to allow the pain in my back to trouble me. When I arrived, I saw that the trains were still running and that there was one heading to Denttingham, albeit several hours late.

You should've seen how packed the train was, Fabien, and how scared and angry people were, but there was no one to blame, except the weather. When the conductor approached me and asked for my ticket, I glanced up at him. I could tell by his expression he had already had several battles with other passengers in order to get them to pay their fare. I wondered if seeing an old woman alone would want to make him take advantage or be more lenient.

'I haven't got a ticket.'

'Ma'am, you need a ticket.'

'Well, sir, I haven't got one.'

'You'll have to buy one.' He lifted his little machine. 'Where are you going?'

'Denttingham, but I've lost my purse.'

He glared at me. He was exasperated – our favourite word. He pulled out a small ticket book that I imagined he had used many times before to punish those who had to choose between food and transport.

'Oh for the love of God,' said a woman across the aisle as the conductor tore a ticket out. 'Don't be a bastard.' There were mumbles of agreement, and the woman, growing in confidence at being the voice of the people, added, 'Have you seen what we've all had to go through the past twenty-four hours? Let the woman get home.'

I inspected my saviour: a younger woman who appeared careworn herself. The conductor glared at the faces watching him before tucking his booklet away and leaving.

'Where are you going?' the Voice of the People asked. It was spoken with concern, and I could see she could tell I had spent the night almost sleeping rough.

'To my son's place. In Denttingham.'

The woman smiled at me. 'Get there safely.'

When I reached Denttingham, I joined the flurry of hoods and umbrellas getting off the train. My back now thumped with a constant ache. I took a seat on a bench and waited for the pain to subside. It didn't. I started calling a series of taxi numbers, hoping that there would be another driver willing to work in this weather.

When one arrived, I told him where to go.

I had forgotten how spectacular your penthouse was, Fabien. I stared up at it. Even in the storm there was an aura of this-is-where-people-who-have-done-well-for-themselves-live about it. There was a garden outside the ground floor that looked like it was pulled from one of those horticulture magazines. I studied it, wondering how even after two weeks of horrific weather it could still look so good. Then it hit me: not once since the storm started had you rung to check if I was alright.

I became exasperated. I gripped the handle of my umbrella until it hurt my palm, but my anger quickly turned into sadness, and I found myself holding back tears.

I lifted my umbrella slightly so I could see the storm. The sky was a pit filled with water tipped upside down, and the dots of rain were flicking my face at every opportunity. I moved forward and my back jolted painfully. I edged towards the nearest bench, which was shielded by a part of the building away from the entrance and shrouded by tall plants. The wind rose even higher, and I decided to stay there behind the defence of the apartments until you came home.

It was dark when you arrived, and despite the storm I could tell by your gait it was you, but your right arm was in a sling. You were carrying an umbrella and were struggling to pull out your key fob. I tried to get up quickly, but my back disagreed, and by the time I had moved, you had managed to get inside.

I knocked on the glass door. There was a man sitting by a desk who I guessed was a security guard, given how he was playing on his phone. He slipped out of his chair and came to the entrance.

'I'm here to see my son.'

My age was enough to disarm him. He asked no questions and let me inside. I neared the lift.

'It's not working,' the security man said. 'The storm's screwed the electrics. You'll have to take the stairs. Can you manage?'

I smiled. 'I can.'

The first flight of stairs was difficult, and a frustrating reminder that I was old. I had to use the handrail to defeat the second flight. I peeped up at the third, aware that there was still a further three until I reached you. More pain. Before, I wasn't sure what I was going to do when I saw you, but now I knew I wanted to hurt you. Physically.

I went on.

It was my back that I felt more than anything else, and as I continued upwards I started to sweat. As I climbed the fourth flight my back burned and stiffened, and I began to doubt myself; maybe you were right: maybe I did need 'a

225

little help'. Maybe I was senile. I allowed those thoughts to sit in my mind while I took a lengthy rest before attempting to conquer the fifth flight.

I was struggling, Fabien. I was using my umbrella as support. My back was on fire. What was I doing here? A bitter old woman, exasperated because her son wouldn't see her … her only son, who told her to abandon her home, forced her into sheltered housing because he didn't want to keep her company, who left her there for months and only showed his face on the news when telling her there would be no end to the worst storm in living memory.

I battled my way up the fifth set of stairs and didn't stop at the top.

When I completed the sixth, I slumped on the final step. I don't know for how long. It might have been five minutes, it might have been twenty, but eventually, I got up.

I knocked. You didn't answer. I knocked harder. I could make out the sound of your footsteps coming closer. There was a click on the door. I waited for you to pull it open, but instead I heard you walking away. Even if you didn't know it was me, to treat any visitor like that said a lot about your character. I pushed it open and saw your silhouette in the centre of your wall-sized windows. When you turned around your demeanour was overly composed, so I knew you weren't prepared to see me.

Neither of us spoke. The room was lit by a single battery-powered lamp.

'Mum?' you said.

I edged forward with the help of my umbrella. 'Fabien.'

You touched your pocket, searching for your phone. 'The warden let you leave in this weather? He shouldn't have.'

'I wanted to surprise you.' I took another step forward.

'Mum, you need to go back.'

'In this weather? No thank you.'

'Mum—'

'No.'

'You're not strong enough to—'

'Fabien,' I shouted. I hadn't raised my voice at you like that in decades. You fell silent. You moved stiffly towards the settee, adjusted the cushions and gestured for me to take a seat. As I lowered myself, you gave me your hand for support.

'Thank you. Sorry for shouting. I've had a long journey, and I'm tired. Avoid asking me questions just yet.'

You nodded.

'I've been watching you on the television. It's the only way I've been able to see you.'

'Mum—'

'No, it's okay. I understand. You're a busy man.' I pointed at you. 'Your country needs you.'

You chuckled, and I quickly forced a laugh. You clasped your hands together. 'You sound good, Mum.'

I put a hand on your knee. 'What happened to your arm?'

You showed me your cast. 'The storm knocked me over.'

I grinned. 'Who's the frail one now?'

For a moment you froze but then swiftly smiled.

'Why didn't you tell me you were coming?'

'I already told you, I wanted to surprise you.' I was

thankful for the darkness of your home and how it helped me to hide how dishevelled I was. 'I've been living in that community for months, and I haven't seen you. I want to know what you've been doing.'

'I don't think it'll interest you.' You squeezed my hand. 'And I'm sorry about that. I've been busy.'

I held my hand up to stop you saying more. 'Don't worry about it. And everything you do interests me.'

You stood up and went to your desk where your laptop was. I let my polite profile drop while your back was facing me, and my eyes seared into the back of your head. When you turned around, I fixed a pleasant expression onto my face. You put your laptop on the table.

'I've been writing this weather blog.'

'Blog?'

'About the storm. I want to explain to people in clear terms what's happening.'

You adjusted the screen so I could see it. I leaned forward and pretended to read it. 'It looks good.'

'It's been successful. I've even thought that maybe … I could write a book, one day. About the weather.'

'That's something you could certainly do.'

You laughed.

I patted your thigh. 'I'm glad you're doing well. What's this blog called?'

You pointed to the large text at the top of the screen, discretely indicating that I was a fool for not noticing the first time.

'The Weatherman,' you said.

'That's appropriate.'

You nodded, staring at your screen. 'I'd reply to the latest comments if I could get the internet to work properly.' The storm whistled outside. 'The electric in the building's acting up. Let me try the lights again.'

'I'll do it. I need to take my coat off anyway.'

'Do you want anything to eat?'

'No, I'm fine.' I moved in a frail fashion to your coat pegs and looked back over my shoulder. Your eyes were still glued to the screen. I put my umbrella up beside yours.

'Mum?'

I didn't answer. Your coat hung on the hook in front of me. Like everything else you owned it was expensive.

'I am happy to see you. You just surprised me, that's all.'

I was quiet. I tried to reply but was so angry that I couldn't. I knew you were lying. My eyes started to water, and behind me I could hear you fumbling around, presumably looking for your phone. What for? Were you going to call the police? Or try to call the warden? I glanced at you; you quickly put your phone down and returned to typing. Without thinking, I found my hand moving and touching the handle of your umbrella. The metal kissed my skin as if to reaffirm my instincts. It was far heavier than mine; a man's brolly, I thought. I didn't peer back at you. I was afraid that if I did, you'd notice what I was doing. I turned slowly as I lifted it off the hook. It was still wet. I sneaked towards you. You turned, and your eyes widened as you saw me thrust the pointed end of your umbrella with all my force towards the side of your head.

You were sprawled on the floor. I was screaming at you. You reached for your temple and found blood.

I was pointing the umbrella at you while trying to stop my bag falling off my shoulder.

'Are you listening?' I shouted. It came out like a hiss. 'Do you know what it was like in there? The people are slow, the water tastes like poison and you know you've been forgotten.' I coughed from exertion. 'You wanted to get rid of me: "Mum, I think you're becoming senile. You're not as strong as you were. You need support."' My voice turned shrill. 'Shoving brochures in my face. Telling me what's best for me.'

You said nothing. I covered my face, and when I removed my hands I was crying. 'If you didn't want to spend your time on me, you could've just said. You didn't have to make me feel like a burden.'

You stared up at me in disbelief while trying to stop your tears from flowing. 'You've just hit me with my own umbrella.'

'Shut up.'

'You left without telling anyone, didn't you?'

'For a weatherman you're not very bright. Of course I did. I walked right out of there.'

You groaned.

'I don't know why you're like this, Fabien, but no son should treat a mother the way you have.'

'You needed help,' you shouted. 'Look what you're doing. Look!'

'Be quiet.'

You started to sit up, but I pointed the umbrella at your injured arm.

'What now then?' you yelled.

'What?'

'What now? What do you want from me? An apology? Are you going to hit me again?'

We stared at each other.

'I don't want an apology.'

You were confused.

'It's too late for that. And I'm not going back to that place. Get up.' I circled around you while aiming the umbrella at you. You watched me as I picked up your laptop with my free hand. 'Transfer everything that's in your bank into my account.' I dumped the laptop on the floor beside your face.

You stared at me.

'I'm never going back to that damn community. I'm getting my own place again, far away from you, and this is going to make sure of it.'

Your mouth fell open. I dug the tip of the umbrella into the cast on your arm, and you shouted out in pain. I didn't know what I was doing, Fabien. It was primitive anger, and I wasn't in control of my own actions, but despite having thoughts telling me this, I didn't stop. You gritted your teeth before turning and entering the details of your bank account into your computer. I sat down. I was breathing heavily. Outside your window the storm was raging. I began mumbling to myself as I caught my breath, waiting for you to finish.

'Why did he put me there?' I wondered. I couldn't be sure if I'd said the words aloud. I noticed movement in the corner of my eye. It was you reaching for your phone on the table.

I screamed and forced myself up before stabbing the umbrella into your injured arm. You were howling and trying to kick me, but you jerked back each time I dug it into the sling. A red blotch started to show through the cast, and I was gasping for breath.

It wasn't until you managed to raise your free hand and scream 'Okay!' that I stopped.

'Do it,' I shouted, gesturing to the computer.

You coughed several times and tried to move. I lifted my bag back onto my shoulder and aimed the umbrella at you again. You shifted onto your side and entered your details. I collapsed back into the chair. It seemed to take forever for the internet to connect momentarily, and I kept a close eye on you to make sure you weren't doing anything else while you waited for the page to load. You shakily made the transfer then rolled onto your back.

The clatter of rain colliding with your windows filled the silence.

Eventually, I crouched down until I was level with you and stroked your hair. 'I'm sorry.'

You were grimacing, and your tears were lost in the blood on the side of your face. I wiped it with my sleeve. You kept your eyes closed.

I dropped your umbrella and struggled up with help of the sofa. I wobbled to the door, took my coat and umbrella off the peg and left.

I caught the next train out of Denttingham. Once again, it was packed. While I waited for it to pull out of the station, I fought back tears and watched the doors with the fear that you or the police would appear. No one did, but my imagination continued to bully me. The night had turned the windows into mirrors, and I stared at my reflection until I became sick of it.

Behind me, a man said a prayer asking for God to spare us, and for the storm to not force the train off the tracks, butchering us all. He then began another prayer in a different language. I wondered how many gods he was trying to reach. I fell asleep before the train had started moving.

I was woken by someone prodding me. It was the conductor – the same one who had attempted to fine me on my way here. The chances of this happening, I thought, were ridiculous, but then nothing was normal any more. He recognised me. He shook his head then turned away. I picked up my purse and told him to hold on. I took my bank card out and hesitated before paying with the money I had taken from you.

I rested my hands on my purse. The light from the laptop belonging to the passenger next to me was reflected in the window. I glanced at their screen and at the article they were reading. *BREAKING NEWS*: BELOVED WEATHER-MAN FABIEN VEIRA BRUTALLY BEATEN was the title. No one truly realises how fast news travels until it involves them. I stared, unblinking, and proceeded to scan the article to see if there was any mention of your mother. There wasn't. I read further. Veira says the attacker was masked. Police are investigating.

My prehistoric phone vibrated. It was a message: Maybe you were right. Please stay safe in this storm. Love, Fabien. I turned my gaze back to the window and watched the rain fall against the glass as water dripped from my eyes onto my hands.

Credits & Acknowledgements

To begin with, I want to thank everyone who has ever taken the time to read and enjoy my stories. Not all of them are mentioned in these pages, but their support of my work has not gone unnoticed, and without their encouragement and feedback, it is unlikely that this collection would have survived long enough to be in your hands today.

Special thanks to the following for their work in helping me create the words on these pages, the stories they tell and the physical book itself: Ray Robinson, who deserves as much gratitude as I can possibly give for the time and advice he provided during the creation of the earliest drafts of this book, his support of my writing in general and for the guidance he has given me over the years; Brett Hackett, for accompanying me on my writing journey not long after it began in 2011 and for reading my writing even when it was ineligible; Aki Schilz, Joe Segdwick and everyone at The Literary Consultancy for being the earliest pillar in my writing career and for being the best kind of validation many writers crave; Okapi Books for being everything an aspiring and innovative publisher should be; Jonathan McAloon, for offering the final adjustments needed to make *The Storm* what it is now; Hannah Grego for her needle-fine editing, for showing me there is always something to be learned in this craft and for providing me with suggestions that have improved my writing in ways that I would have been unable to without her; Arantza Pardo for creating the painting and artwork for the collection, for being a pleasure to work with as well as an inspiration; Nathan Ryder, for his patience with this book's design, his enthusiasm, kindness, talent and work ethic; my twin brother, Kazem Balogun, for having the endlessly fascinating ability to make things to come to life and for using his talents make this collection come alive through animation; Christian Brett, for his extensive knowledge, beautiful typesetting and his willingness to explain every step of what was a foreign process for me; Richard Sheehan for his experienced proofing of the book and for ensuring that the reader's journey is as seamless as possible; TJ Books for being one of the most excellent and most helpful printers in the UK; Blank Street Writers, lastly, for being an invaluable resource and for helping me over the past several years to become the writer that I am today.

Special thanks to Geoff Briggs, Bryan Dramiga, Taiwo and Kehinde Balogun, Nathan Stacey, Jade Yiu, Prince Brown, Désirée Reynolds, Brian Lewis of Longbarrow Press, Bryony Doran, Bill Allerton and Hasan Mahmood for their important contributions and time to my writing and my aspirations.

Acknowledgements go out to the following for their significant and unwavering support of my work in the years leading up to the release of this collection:

Adam Bakri
Dayo Balogun
Laurence Baulder
Louise Briggs
Charlie Burns
Kit Caless
Kayle-Yves Chrouch
Ailsa Cox
Ian Daley
Will Denniff
Brunetty Dilhoulou
James Euinton
Kirsty Fairweather
Peter Hiscock
John Kamara
Drew King
Megan Klodnicki
Ishmael Lammy
Joanne Leeman
Carl Loftus
Tony Millward
Shivan Mistry
Mohammed Omar
Andrei Pambuccian
David Powell
Phil Richardson

239

Sean Robinson
Karen Roe
Jamie Ryder
Charlie Sellings
Rider Shafique
Off the Shelf
Raluca de Soleil
Cut A Long Story
Steve Suggit
Joshua Swaby
Now Then
Rebecca Thirkettle
Rose Tran
Bethany Turner
Laura Turner
Edgehill University
Sheffield Hallam University
Wasafiri
Benjamin Webster
Richard Wilde
Wodwo
Warda Yassin
Signposts South Yorkshire

Copyright Acknowledgements